Praise for Mario Bencastro's
The Tree of Life / Árbol de la vida

"Bencastro relies heavily upon sarcasm and humor to deliver his powerful message . . . *The Tree of Life* shows readers a side of the struggle in El Salvador on a human, daily level."

—*Copley News Service*

"[A] skillful blend of fantasy with reality . . . *The Tree of Life: Stories of Civil War* contains twelve of Bencastro's fictions, and the work is uniformly strong . . . 'Once Upon a River,' the final fiction in the book, is also the longest and most powerful . . . [It] constitutes a short novella which shows the absolute savagery of the civil war while at the same time showcasing Bencastro's considerable talents for drawing character through the medium of a minor literary masterwork. Steadily, Mario Bencastro has been building a solid reputation as a writer . . . Susan Giersbach Rascón's fine translation makes this first English edition of the book a memorable event."

—*The Texas Review*

"The passion and politics of the civil war in El Salvador, the blight of political strife, and social injustice color this richly textured short story collection . . . Turmoil, intrigue, and suffering have been captured and universalized in these beautifully wrought tales . . . Not journalistic reportage but magical realism at its best, the stories in *The Tree of Life* are deceptively simple, linear, and fresh."

—*El Mundo Latino*

Odyssey to the North

Other Works by Mario Bencastro from Arte Público Press

A Shot in the Cathedral

Disparo en la catedral

The Tree of Life: Stories of Civil War

Árbol de la vida: Historias de la guerra civil

Critical Praise for Mario Bencastro's
A Shot in the Cathedral / Disparo en la catedral

"Bencastro's dramatic, powerful first novel focuses on the military *coup d'etat* in El Salvador in 1979 . . . A vivid newsreel of a country disintegrating."

—*Publishers Weekly*

"A skillful balance between journalistic reportage and a subjective focus on the lives of ordinary people afflicted by political upheaval . . . [Relates] a vivid and engrossing sequence of events whose deeply involved observer—an average man who unaccountably becomes both newspaper reporter and hero—makes powerfully real for us the human dimensions of war's phlegmatic impersonality."

—*Kirkus Reviews*

"One of Latin America's particular and notable contributions to world literature has been the political novel . . . Latin American narrative has depicted political turmoil in artful and often innovative ways. Such is the case with Bencastro's *A Shot in the Cathedral* . . . Bencastro persuasively reports, describes, and synthesizes the hopelessness and transcendence of the brutal political struggle in El Salvador."

—*Choice*

(Please turn the page for more rave reviews)

More Praise for
A Shot in the Cathedral / Disparo en la catedral

"Susan Giersbach Rascón has deftly translated this technically sophisticated novel, which has multiple narrators and ably mixes fiction with history."

—*Multicultural Review*

"*Una época de terror y miedo es revisida con intensidad en esta corta pero penetrante novela histórica del escritor salvadoreño Mario Bencastro . . . Un excelente cronista de su tiempo. Esta edición, disponible tanto en español como en inglés, permito al lector hispano disfrutar del estilo vivaz de este gran narrador.*

[A time of terror and fear is revisited with intensity in this brief but penetrating historical novel by Salvadoran writer Mario Bencastro . . . An excellent chronicle of its time. This edition, available in both Spanish and English, allows the Hispanic reader to enjoy the vigorous style of this great storyteller.]"

—*People Magazine en español*

Odyssey to the North

Mario Bencastro

Translated by Susan Giersbach Rascón

Arte Público Press
Houston, Texas
1998

This volume is made possible through grants from the National Endowment for the Arts (a federal agency), Andrew W. Mellon Foundation, the Lila Wallace-Reader's Digest Fund and the City of Houston through The Cultural Arts Council of Houston, Harris County.

Recovering the past, creating the future

Arte Público Press
University of Houston
452 Cullen Performance Hall
Houston, Texas 77204-2004

Bencastro, Mario.
    [Odisea al norte. English]
    Odyssey to the north / Mario Bencastro; translated by Susan Giersbach Rascón.
    p.   cm.
    ISBN 1-55885-256-5 (pbk. : alk. paper)
    I. Rascón, Susan Giersbach. II. Title.
PQ7539.2.B4603513   1998
863—dc21   98-28339
                                                                 CIP

⊚ The paper used in this publication meets the requirements of the American National Standard for Information Sciences—Permanence of Paper for Printed Library Materials, ANSI Z39.48-1984.

1 2 3 4 5 6 7 8 9 0   11 10 9 8 7 6 5 4 3 2

Author's Note

I would like to acknowledge all the people and institutions who, with their testimonies, ideas, writings, and reports, assisted in the realization of this work: especially the writer Carlos Quiroa; attorney Susan Giersbach Rascón; sociologist Segundo Montes; writer Carlos Matías Gutiérrez ("Milonga del fusilado"); writer Consuelo Hernández; the newspapers *El Tiempo Latino* (Carlos M. Cabán) and *The Arizona Daily Star* (Rob Levin) and the Library of Congress of the United States.

This is a work of fiction. Certain events have been commingled with situations and characters of my own invention to create this narrative. With the exception of the content of some newspaper articles, any similarity to actual events, places, or people (living or dead) is coincidental.

M.B.

They came from distant places
Carrying their dreams
Seeking the land of gold.

Many perished in the crossing
Others reached strange cities
They found hope
They began a new life.

Some continued the journey
Beyond the horizon.

1

"It's going to be a beautiful day here in Washington!" exclaimed the voice on the radio. "Clear blue skies, seventy degrees, sunny with no threat of rain. A perfect spring day!"

Two policemen were making their rounds in the Adams Morgan district, the windows of their patrol car open to receive the cool breeze which caressed the groves of trees in Rock Creek Park, carrying the perfume of the multicolored flowers outlined against the delicate blue sky.

The metallic voice coming over the transmitter from headquarters shook them out of their deep thoughts, ordering them to proceed immediately to a building on Harvard Street, across from the zoo, just a few minutes away.

When they arrived on the scene, they had to fight their way through the crowd of residents who had come running in response to the desperate shouts of a woman.

They ordered the people to move aside and then they saw the cause of the commotion: a smashed body stuck to the hot cement. The cranium was demolished. The facial features were disfigured by a grimace of pain. The eyes were still open, with an enigmatic gaze. The arms and legs were arranged incoherently, not at all in the normal symmetry of the human body. One leg was bent with the foot up by the neck. One shoulder was completely separated from the body, as if it had been chopped off.

"Spiderman!" someone exclaimed.

One of the policemen approached the man who had shouted and said to him, "Hey, show some respect; this is no joke!"

The man turned around and walked away, hanging his head. But as soon as he was out of the officer's reach, he turned around and screamed, "Spiderman! Spiderman!" and took off running toward the zoo, where he hid among some bushes.

The policeman started to chase him, but settled for insulting the man silently, biting his lip to keep the words from escaping.

"Is there anyone here who knows the victim?" asked the other officer, scrutinizing the group of curious onlookers with an indecisive expression.

No one dared to say a word.

"You?" he asked a brown-skinned man. "Do you know him?"

"I don't speak English," the man answered fearfully.

"*¿Tú, conocer, muerto?*" insisted the officer, stammering in thickly accented Spanish.

"I don't speak Spanish either," said the man in broken English. "I'm from Afghanistan."

The policeman appeared utterly disconcerted at the people's silence. The loud sound of a lion's roar came from the zoo.

Finally, a woman approached the men in uniform and, in an anxious voice, stated, "I was coming home from the store and when I was climbing the stairs to go into the building I heard a scream . . . Then I saw the shape of a man in the sky . . . With his arms stretched out like he was flying . . . But he came crashing down headfirst on the cement . . . He was just a ball of flesh and blood . . . He didn't move anymore . . ."

The people listened openmouthed as the terrified woman described what had happened. One of the officers took down all the details in a small notebook. A reporter took countless photographs per second, as if unable to satisfy his camera.

The shouts of "Spiderman! Spiderman!" were heard again, but this time they were completely ignored.

Calixto was among the spectators, stunned, terrified, and livid, unable to say a word about the tragedy, incapable of testifying that as they were washing the windows outside the eighth floor, the rope tied around his companion's waist broke. Calixto feared they would blame him for the death and he would end up in jail, if not deported for being undocumented. "And then," he thought, "who would support my family?"

The superintendent of the building was observing the scene from the lobby. He was not willing to talk either. He feared he would lose his job for permitting windows at that height to be washed without proper equipment for such a dangerous task. It would come out that he employed undocumented workers and paid them only a third of what cleaning companies usually charged.

The ambulance siren sounded in the neighborhood with such shrillness that it frightened the animals in the zoo. The lion roared as if protesting all the commotion.

The paramedics made their way through the crowd and laid a stretcher on the ground near the body. After a brief examination, one of them said dryly, "He's dead," confirming what everyone already knew.

"Who is he?" one of the paramedics asked the police. "What's his name?"

"No one knows," responded the officer. "Nobody seems to recognize him."

"He looks Hispanic," stated the other paramedic, observing the body closely.

"Maybe he's from Central America," said a woman, clutching her purse to her chest. "A lot of them live in this neighborhood . . . You know, they come here fleeing the wars in their countries . . ."

"If he's not from El Salvador, he must be from Guatemala," agreed one of the paramedics. "Although now they're coming from all over: Bolivia, Peru, Colombia. We used to be the ones who invaded their countries; now they invade ours. Soon Washington will look like Latin America."

"Poor devils," said the other paramedic. "They die far from home, like strangers."

Meanwhile, in the zoo, the lion's loud roar was answered by that of the lioness. The pair of felines, oblivious to the conflicts going on around them, were consummating the reproduction of their species, part of the ancient rites of spring.

The paramedics put the body into the ambulance. The policemen left. The crowd dispersed. A strange red stain remained on the cement.

3

Calixto entered the zoo and began to walk absent-mindedly among the cages, thinking about his co-worker who just half an hour ago had been telling him that he had already bought his ticket to return to his country, where he planned to open a grocery store with the money he had saved from five years of hard work in the United States.

Suddenly Calixto realized that in a matter of minutes he had become unemployed. Despair seized him as he remembered that it had taken him a month and a half of constant searching to get the window washing job.

He spent the entire day at the zoo and, as he agonized over whether to return to his country or stay in Washington, he walked from one end of the zoo to the other several times. When they closed the park, he began to walk down long streets with strange names, until finally night fell and he had no choice but to return to the place where he lived, a tiny one-bedroom apartment occupied by twenty people.

"At least I'm alive," he said to himself. "That's good enough for me."

2

Calixto got up early and, without eating breakfast, left the apartment to look for work. He stopped at several businesses along Columbia Road where, according to the comments he had heard at the apartment, Spanish was spoken. But they gave him no hope of a job because he did not have a Social Security card or a green card. Nevertheless, he did not give up; he knew he would find something. "Even if it's cleaning bathrooms, it doesn't matter; in this country people aren't ashamed to do anything."

To alleviate his desperation a little, he paused in front of the window of a clothing store. His gaze fell on the tiny alligator that adorned one of the shirts, and the price of the shirt startled him. He remembered that in his country they made clothing like that. In his neighborhood, in fact, everyone went around with that little figure on their chests. It made no difference that the crocodile faded with the first washing, came loose with the second, and that after the third washing nothing was left of the reptile but a hole in the shirt. Calixto realized it was pointless to dream about new things when he did not even have a job, and he continued walking along Columbia Road. When he reached the corner of 18th Street, he decided to go into McDonald's. A fellow countryman from Intipucá whom Calixto had met at the apartment had heard that there were job opportunities there. He noticed a dark-skinned man who looked Latin American picking up papers from the floor and wiping off tables. He approached him, and asked in Spanish, "Do you know if they're hiring here?"

The man responded with a smile and strange gestures.

"Work," repeated Calixto. "Washing dishes or anything."

But the man did not understand him because he was Indian and did not speak Spanish.

"Go to Hell!" said Calixto, frustrated because the man did nothing but smile at him.

He left McDonald's in despair and stood for a moment on the corner, unable to decide whether to walk down 18th Street or continue on Columbia Road. The memory of his home in El Salvador suddenly flooded his mind, the memory of the life of hunger and misery he led there, and he realized that little or nothing had changed for him. He was suffering in this country too; and he wasn't sure if it was better to be here or there. What he did know was that he was out of work, and that he did not even have enough money in his pocket to buy a beer to drown the sorrow of feeling lonely and abandoned in a strange land.

He continued wandering down Columbia Road, then took Connecticut Avenue and walked to Dupont Circle Park. He sat down on a bench to watch the transients and elderly people who were sitting in the sun throwing bread crumbs to the pigeons. He noticed several beggars dragging large bundles which apparently represented their belongings but to him looked like garbage. They reminded him of Old Rag, one of the many beggars in his neighborhood, who also dragged big bags of garbage through the streets, and Calixto concluded that misery was everywhere. He consoled himself with the thought that at least he was healthy and had a family, even though they were now far away.

He returned to the apartment after dark and was pleasantly surprised to find his cousin Juancho there.

"Tomorrow I'm starting work in a hotel," said Juancho. "Come with me. I've been told they need a lot of people because a few days ago the *migra* raided the place and arrested a lot of the employees."

"Well let's go!" said Calixto. "Maybe I'll get a job too."

"I'll meet you tomorrow at the corner of 18th and Columbia Road, at 8 a.m. sharp," said Juancho.

"I'll be there," said Calixto. "For sure."

He said goodbye to his cousin and went to bed with his stomach empty but his soul full of hope.

The next day when they went to the hotel, a manager told them they did need people urgently, and they could start work that very moment.

"The misfortune of some is the good fortune of others," Calixto said to himself.

They immediately put on their uniforms and went into the kitchen.

"We look like nurses," said Calixto. "I've never dressed in white before."

"Never say never," laughed Juancho. "In this country the strangest things happen."

Used to surviving in difficult situations, Calixto was an extremely optimistic person. This had given him the courage necessary to leave his homeland and come to a strange country. As they said back home, he "didn't turn up his nose at anything," because Calixto was a capable man.

3

(In the kitchen of a hotel restaurant. Calixto, Caremacho and Juancho chat while they wash dishes.)

I came to the United States because the situation in El Salvador got too dangerous.

Me too. And things were so difficult that it was impossible to find work.

Caremacho, do you remember what happened in our neighborhood?

Of course!

(Calixto appears quite intrigued.) What happened?

Well, after Quique, a friend of ours, was killed, the situation got real dangerous, and everyone was afraid.

But, what happened?

One morning Quique's body was found. He had been tortured.

They say that he had already been arrested once before.

He was blacklisted.

But why?

Because he had been fingered by someone.

Part of the problem was alcohol. He was more drunk than rum itself.

That's for sure. And that time, as usual, Quique had gone to the Three Skulls bar to have a few drinks.

And he left there practically crawling.

He lost control of himself. And later, in Doña Chica's diner, he began to talk too much.

A slip of the tongue. And, like they say, "The walls have ears," and someone reported him.

What a fool.

They say that when he saw the police he tried to escape. He fled like a bat out of Hell.

But he didn't make it. They got him anyway.

But Quique was brave.

That's for sure. Brave, stubborn and brash.

And at the moment of truth he pulled a knife.

And in the end he fought them off with punches, kicks and even bites.

But even so, he wasn't able to save himself.

And he died right there.

From then on all of us were very careful.

Yeah. I said to myself, "That's the last straw; I'm getting out of here before the same thing happens to me!"

And you, why?

Because Quique and I were good friends. They might think I was involved in the same things he was.

I didn't come to the United States out of fear, but because I was tired of going hungry, of constantly looking and never finding even one damn job. So I borrowed some money for the trip and came to try my luck.

I did the same thing. And look, here I am.

And you, Calixto, why are you here?

One of these days I'll tell you my story. The important thing is we're all here now.

We aren't starving to death anymore.

And we aren't in danger of being put in jail because of political problems.

Although things aren't perfect here either.

You're right, Calixto.

4

When several men arrived at the family's room looking for Calixto, Lina, his wife, was at her friend Hortensia's apartment, at the other end of the building. A neighbor came running to tell them.

"They're looking for Don Calixto to arrest him!"

"Arrest him for what?" asked Lina, in startled disbelief.

"They say he's an enemy of the government!"

"Don't go back to your apartment!" interrupted Hortensia.

"Sweet Name of Jesus!" screamed Lina, terrified. "What are we going to do?"

"The first thing is to warn Calixto! Leave the children here and run to where he's working!"

Lina left immediately, wishing she were a bird, able to fly to Calixto before they surprised him there. In her distress she ignored the burning sun which baked her temples and she hurried even faster, knowing that her husband's very life depended on her. Her children had remained behind, frightened and crying, but she was thankful they were in good hands. Hortensia was the godmother of all three of them. The children had all been baptized together in the church in their slum, a ramshackle shelter on a vacant lot, surrounded by garbage, dust, flies, and stray dogs. There, on an improvised altar, a priest who was very popular in that neighborhood used to celebrate Sunday Mass, the same cheerful priest whose tortured body was found later under the church's canopy.

Sweating profusely beneath the intense sun, Lina finally arrived at the place where Calixto worked. Seeing his wife's terrified expression, he knew immediately that something was wrong, and he ran to meet her.

"They're looking for you!" she said, her cry muffled by distress and exhaustion. "Someone reported you as an enemy of the government!"

"It can't be! I'm not involved in politics, you know that!"

"You have to get out of here and hide, before they find you!"

"But it must be a mistake!" insisted Calixto. "Or someone's slandering me. One or the other."

"It doesn't matter; you've been reported!"

"Yes, but . . ."

He could not finish what he was going to say because the shout of "Calixto, someone's looking for you!" frightened him to the point of stealing his words.

"Go!" his wife begged him.

"Where?"

"To Lencho's house!"

Quick as a cat, Calixto jumped into the bushes and disappeared. Lina left too, the way she had come, back down the road she used to travel every day at noon to bring Calixto his lunch, in a pewter lunch pail that held their everyday food: rice, beans, tortillas and a piece of fresh cheese. She used to sit with him while he ate hastily, both of them seated on a piece of wood, among machines, bags of cement and piles of sand, at the construction site of one of the many new buildings that were going up at that time in the capital. He would eat silently, hungry and tired, worried about the job, which was hard, poorly paid, and in a few weeks would end. Her worry was the children she had left playing in the yard in Hortensia's care.

"Thank the Lord they didn't catch him," she thought as she returned home. Then she remembered the anguished expressions on her children's faces when she left them, and she hurried until she was running, but stopped close to the building before proceeding cautiously to Hortensia's apartment. She heard her friend's voice consoling the children, who were crying. She breathed a sigh of relief, went in and embraced them as gently as she could. They stopped crying, feeling safe and secure again in their mother's arms.

The fear of being captured pushed Calixto to hurry through the city without tiring. He finally arrived in the neighborhood he was looking for, but desperation had clouded his memory and he could not remember how to get to his friend's home. Lencho was an old friend of Calixto's. Together they had left the remote village where they had lived in huts made of straw and adobe and cultivated small plots of mountainous terrain, to seek a better life in the capital. A short time later, their village was completely destroyed in a bloody battle between the army and rebel forces.

When he finally recognized the building where Lencho lived, Calixto found his apartment locked.

"Don Lencho won't be long," said a neighbor. "Wait here if you like."

"Thank you."

Calixto sat down on a wooden stool and only then did he realize how exhausted he was and that his entire body was bathed in sweat. "I'm sweating like a horse," he thought, as he observed the tenants coming and going and listened to the jumbled sounds of music from many radios mixed with the residents' voices.

Old Lencho appeared at the gate and ambled across the yard in his usual slow way. When he saw Calixto, he was surprised at the worry on his face. "As if he'd seen the devil," he thought as he opened the door.

"Hi, Calixto," said Lencho. "What a surprise to see you here!"

He invited Calixto to sit down on a folding canvas chair and served him a glass of cool water from an earthen jug. Although Calixto had not said a word, the old man sensed that his friend was in trouble.

"Tell me," he said to him. "How can I help you?"

Between long drinks of water, Calixto told him the whole story.

"You've been lucky, my friend," said the old man. "Lucky they didn't get you; if they had, who knows what would have become of you by now . . ."

"That's for sure," said Calixto, convinced. "How lucky I was! Thank God!"

"Don't worry about anything else; you can stay here as long as necessary. And if you want, bring Lina and the children too."

"Thank you so much, Lencho; you don't know how much I appreciate this."

"No reason to thank me. Today for you, tomorrow for me, as the saying goes."

Calixto breathed a sigh of relief. Now the only thing that oppressed his spirit was not knowing how his wife and children were. But he firmly believed that Lina somehow would find a way to protect them. "There's no one like my Lina," he said to himself with pride, and thought about how his wife, hardworking, faithful and resolute, was one of the few blessings life had bestowed upon him. These thoughts comforted him somewhat on this day when, because of a simple mistake, or perhaps slander, his destiny had taken an abrupt and unexpected turn, which endangered his existence and that of his loved ones. And now what? What was he going to do?

"For right now, nothing," said Old Lencho. "Stay here and lay low for a few days. Don't even stick your nose out. We'll see what we can do to straighten this out."

5

(In the kitchen. Calixto, Juancho, Caremacho, Chele Chile, Cali.)

Housing is a real problem here. When I arrived in Washington, the first few months I stayed in an apartment where there were already a lot of people living.

(A Chilean cook's helper enters; his nickname is Chele Chile.) How many people were living there?

Twenty.

(Cali, a Colombian waiter, enters.) In how many rooms?

Just one bedroom.

Twenty, in a one-bedroom apartment?

Damn! You were crammed in like sardines!

There were seven women, four men, six children, two elderly people and one sixteen-year-old girl.

You must have slept one on top of the other.

Even walking was difficult, especially at night, because we would trip over each other.

(Caremacho, jokingly.) Calixto bumped into the others because he was crawling around in the dark looking for the sixteen-year-old girl.

(Cali, surprised.) That's like being in jail. I mean, I've never been in jail, but I imagine that's what it's like.

There was no privacy. The families would gather in the corners of the apartment and arrange their belongings there.

And where did you all sleep?

People would sleep and eat in the same little corner. They would discuss their family matters in a whisper, but everyone could hear.

How could you all share a bathroom?

We always had to wait in line. Maybe because the situation made us nervous, people were always sick to their stomach and used the bathroom often.

Didn't it get plugged up?

Of course it did! And that really complicated things.

(*Cali, with curiosity.*) What did you do then?

Well, we would use plastic bags or newspaper and throw everything into the incinerator. The one who was actually renting the apartment used to say that the building superintendent complained of the terrible stench that filled the building when he burned the garbage.

What floor was the apartment on?

The fifth. And some of those who had just crossed the border wouldn't look out the window.

Why not?

They were afraid they'd fall out of the building and end up with their guts all over the street.

Come on! How can someone be afraid of falling out of a building?

I believe it. I've met a lot of people who come from the country and most of them haven't even been to the capital of their country, haven't seen a building with more than one floor, much less lived on a fifth floor.

That's for sure. Many of us come directly from our little towns.

Imagine then what a tremendous surprise it must be to come from a remote place where there isn't even electricity and, suddenly, find yourself in a country as advanced as this one. It has to be a big shock.

That's right. And many of us aren't prepared for it.

But, as time went on, people became convinced that the windows were secure and that looking out of them was the only way to observe the new world in which they were living.

And you, Calixto, how did you feel back then?

Let's just say not so well.

Why?

Because the first months were very difficult for me, and I wasn't expecting that, because I arrived with my head full of a whole bunch of fantasies.

The same thing happened to me. In Colombia I had been told the story that here everyone made a lot of money and that it was really easy to buy expensive things, like cars, and enjoy life in the company of blonde, beautiful women.

I didn't have that idea. My only desire was to find a job, get some money together and send it to my family, so they could pay someone to bring them here. But several months went by and I began to lose hope living in that apartment that stunk like dirty feet, old sweat, rancid farts and shit.

(*Loud laughter. The head cook, a German they nicknamed Hitler, approaches the group, shouting.*) Hey, jerk, get back to work! (*He exits.*)

Shut up, Hitler!

"Jerk" is that German's favorite word.

It's the only word he knows in Spanish, and when he gets mad he uses it to insult everyone.

Tell us more about the apartment, Calixto.

In the midst of that asphyxiating crowd, I thought that if this was the United States, then I had made a mistake . . .

And the children? How could they play?

They were the ones I felt the most sorry for, because they weren't allowed to play or run for fear that the neighbors would find out that so many people were living in that apartment. They would cry silently, day and night, and those sad sounds would put all our nerves on edge because, besides the desperation caused by being crowded together in the apartment, we still had not recovered from the nightmares and horrors we had suffered during the long trip.

One goes through hard times here.

From the moment we left El Salvador we didn't have one tranquil moment. And afterward, confined in that dark and stinking apartment, I wondered if all the sacrifice was worth it, and sometimes I thought maybe it would have been better to stay in my country and resign myself to running the risk of being arrested.

And why were they going to arrest you?

Maybe this Calixto was a guerrilla.

Lies that had been told about me.

6

Night descended over the city, darkening the landscape and the spirits of its inhabitants. It was the moment when the shadows slid through streets, ravines and roofs to begin nocturnal rituals.

Nighttime was horrifying in the city because it belonged not to people but to the shadows that played with the destiny of human beings.

"What a horrible night," thought Calixto as he took off his worn shoes and lay down on the straw sleeping mat that Old Lencho had provided for him. He thought about many things whose images mixed with concern for his loved ones, forming a whirlwind in his mind.

The loud snoring of the old man made it even more difficult for Calixto to fall asleep. He felt like he was swimming in a great void, suspended in the darkness of the room in the midst of the silence which from time to time was broken by the splash of a toad jumping in the pools in the yard, by the noise of distant gunshots or by the echoes of explosions, noises typical at night in a city where the shadows reigned, from which no one was safe when it was his turn to be devoured by them.

It was also nighttime in Hortensia's apartment, where Lina and her children were staying. Lina tossed and turned in bed, tortured by the darkness and by her anguish. What had become of Calixto? Had they caught and arrested him? Had he been able to find Lencho?

Hortensia sensed that the uncertainty was tormenting her friend and whispered, "Don't worry, Lina; Calixto is fine."

"Oh, Niña Hortensia, only God knows."

"Yes, he's all right, believe me. You'll see; tomorrow you'll find him safe and sound."

"I hope so," said Lina, sighing. "May Saint Martin of Porres take care of him. My little saint who is black like the night."

She said a prayer which she repeated countless times with the fervent desire that her words would somehow speed up the time, frighten away the shadows, dissolve the night, so she could travel across the city and be reunited with Calixto.

And she could not tell for sure whether her wish had come true, but she felt that the night passed in a flash. It was as if her prayer, through its many repetitions, had worked magic, creating the sun to swallow up the night.

The knocking on the door awakened Calixto. Lencho was still snoring. "He's sleeping like a log," thought Calixto, and he had to shake Lencho several times to wake him up.

"Someone's knocking on the door," he whispered into his ear.

"I'll be right there!" said the old man. "Who could it be so early?"

He uncovered himself and stood up slowly, signaling to Calixto to be quiet and hide under the bed, as he put on his pants and went to unlock the door.

"Good morning," said the young man who had knocked.

"Oh, it's Toño. What are you doing here so early?"

"I came to say goodbye."

"To say goodbye? You're going back to the village? If I were you, I wouldn't do that," said the old man, inviting him in. "I wouldn't go back if they paid me."

"No, Don Lencho, I'm not going back to our village."

"Where, then?"

"To the United States."

"What are you saying?"

"Yes, Mister Lencho," responded Toño in English, jokingly. "To the North."

"Go on! Those are serious words," said the old man, knocking on the wooden frame of the bed.

Toño was surprised to see Calixto come out from under the bed. Lencho explained: "This is Calixto, a neighbor of ours from the village, a friend of mine and of your father."

"Sure, I remember him," said Toño.

"I recognize you too," said Calixto. "You're Matías' cousin, aren't you?"

"That's right," said Toño.

"Don't tell anyone he's hiding here," warned the old man, "because the authorities are after him."

"Holy Father!" said Toño. "If they find him, who knows what'll happen to him."

"Yeah, man," agreed Calixto. "And the worst thing is I'm not even involved in political things. Who knows who the hell fingered me? And now I don't know what to do. I need to work to support my wife and three children, but I can't do anything if I have to be on the run."

"He can't even leave the house," said the old man. "He's really in a big mess!"

"If I could go back to our village," said Calixto. "at least there I could work the land."

"Nothing is left of the village but a pile of rocks," said Toño. "My uncle Demetrio went to see it and he came back crushed, crying, saying they had even destroyed the cemetery where our grandparents were buried."

"Not even the dead are safe from this war," commented Lencho. "Much less the living."

"I don't know what the hell I'm going to do now," said Calixto. "I feel trapped."

"If I were you, I'd go to the United States," said Toño. "Try your luck. If you stay here, your life is in danger."

"The United States? What's it like there?"

"Well, I don't know what it's like," said Toño. "But my cousin has told me it's a very big, powerful, rich country, where there are opportunities for people who are determined to work hard."

"Here, this war shows no signs of ending," said Lencho. "With each passing day the economy gets worse. Even the rich people have left the country."

"And the poor just get poorer," said Calixto.

"That's exactly why I'm leaving," said Toño. "I haven't been able to find a decent job. And if I'm not careful, I'll end up a soldier, fighting a war I don't understand but that can kill me."

"But, how are you going? And where?" asked Lencho. "Because it's not just a matter of grabbing your bags and saying you're going. You have to know how."

"I know a man who arranges trips, a *coyote* . . ."

"A what?" asked Calixto. "Isn't a coyote an animal?"

"Yes, but that's also what they call the people who know how to enter the United States without documents."

"And why don't people just get papers to enter the United States legally?" asked Lencho.

"Because, to give you a visa, the U. S. Embassy has a lot of requirements that poor people like us can't meet," said Toño. "Like having a good job, money saved in the bank, good personal references, a round trip ticket, proof that the people we're going to visit in the United States are well-off financially and reside there legally, and other requirements. But, with a *coyote*, you can do it without so much paperwork."

"Do you know anyone over there?" asked Calixto.

"Well, my cousin Matías went over there a year ago with the help of other relatives who've lived in Washington for three years. They work as masons, and they make good money. Juancho, another friend from our village, works in a restaurant washing dishes."

"I didn't know Juancho was there!" said Calixto. "He's my cousin."

"And how much do the *coyotes* charge for the trip?" asked Lencho.

"It depends."

"On what?" asked Calixto, interested.

"It depends on the deal you make with the guide. In my case it's four hundred dollars up front and, when we arrive, my cousins will pay the rest: four hundred more. And this trip is one of the cheapest. They say that others charge a lot more."

"Eight hundred dollars is a fortune," said Calixto.

"It sure is," agreed Lencho. "Not just anyone can come up with that kind of money."

"Usually people only get enough to pay for the trip to Mexico, and the rest is paid by a relative who lives in the United States before they cross the border."

"But even that way, it's not so easy to come by four hundred dollars," said Lencho.

"That's right," nodded Toño. "I was lucky that my cousin sent me the money to make the first payment."

"Great," said Calixto. "It looks like you have everything all set."

"Thanks to God and to my cousin," said Toño. "Well, I have to go now," he said, heading toward the door. "We're leaving for Guatemala tomorrow at noon. I still have to say goodbye to a lot of relatives. See you."

"Listen, Toño," said Lencho. "How do you get a *coyote*?"

"Every day there are ads in the newspapers," said Toño. "A lot of them even offer to pick you up at your home and drop you off personally at the address of a friend or relative in any part of the United States. But I'll leave you a phone number, just in case."

"Leave me the names and addresses of your cousins in Washington too. Who knows, maybe I'll decide to take a trip there too. My body is old, but my heart is young!"

The young man wrote the information on a piece of paper that he gave to Lencho.

"Here it is. Oh, and before I forget, I want to tell you that José, my uncle on my mother's side, is also arranging a trip. He already found a guide and they're leaving a week from today."

"Does José still live in Colonia Manzano?" asked Lencho.

"That's right," responded Toño. "Well then, I'll get going," he said, shaking the old man's hand. "Goodbye."

"God bless you, young man. Take care, and behave yourself; after all, that doesn't cost you anything."

"Goodbye," said Toño, shaking Calixto's hand. "Maybe we'll see you over there. You know you can count on me if you need anything."

"Thank you, Toño," said Calixto. "Take care, and good luck."

The young man disappeared through the clothing hanging on the lines in the yard. The two men were left standing in the semi-darkness of the apartment, which suddenly was illuminated by the sun's rays filtering in through the holes in the tile roof.

7

(Kitchen. Calixto, Juancho, Caremacho, Cali, and Chele Chile discuss an article in the newspaper which, bearing the rather sensational headline "Hell in Mount Pleasant," declared: "In the basement of an abandoned house on Irving Street, four adults and one minor died consumed by the flames of a fire whose origin has been impossible to determine. Nor has the identity of the victims been established. According to preliminary investigations by the authorities, they were possibly of Latin American origin.")

The Wizard slept there. He must have died in the fire.

And who was the Wizard, Calixto?

Where was he from?

I never knew. But I do know that sometimes he would speak in a strange language that some said was Quechua, others said Mayan.

Maybe he was speaking Aymará. Lately a lot of people have come to Washington from the Andes Mountains in Bolivia and Peru. In those regions they still speak the ancient languages like Quechua and Aymará.

Wasn't he that bum who used to spit at people?

That's the one!

That guy was totally crazy.

They say he'd ask people for money and, when they didn't give him any, he'd spit at them.

One night I had to sleep in that basement that burned.

This Calixto would sleep anywhere!

Beggars can't be choosers . . . I remember that huge rats would come out in the basement.

Didn't they bite you?

Luckily they didn't. Otherwise that would have been the end of me, because people say they carry rabies.

And the Wizard, did they bite him?

Yeah, but he said nothing affected him.

He was a sick person.

He looked Indian.

(*Tadeo, a Peruvian, the hotel plumber enters the kitchen, and Chele Chile, his friend, teases him.*) Maybe he was Peruvian. Peruvians are ugly.

(*Tadeo, calmly.*) Chileans aren't ugly. They're horrible!

(*They all laugh.*) The time I slept in the basement, I heard the Wizard say he was born in the mountains.

The Andes, maybe?

Or possibly he came from the mountains of Guatemala. There are lots of Guatemalans in Washington now too.

The truth is that now there are people from all over Latin America here.

Who knows where the Wizard was from. He used to say that he belonged to an ancient indigenous race, that all his people had been exterminated, and he was the last survivor.

And why did they call him the Wizard?

Because he used to do magic tricks.

I met him before he went crazy. We were working in a restaurant and people were kind of afraid of him because of the strange things he did.

Like what?

He could make things move just by staring at them. The knives and forks would bend.

What a weird guy.

Once the *migra* raided the restaurant and caught everyone except him.

How's that? Did he escape from them?

No. According to what he told me later, he made himself invisible, and when the agents entered the kitchen they didn't see him, even though he was right there!

Then, it's impossible for him to have died in the fire, because he could disappear before the flames trapped him.

(*Caremacho chimes in.*) Or he could have put out the fire with his magic!

It could be. But the time the rats bit him, I heard him say that the only thing that could harm him was fire.

Just imagine how the Wizard died. And to come so far just to end up burned to a crisp in the basement of an abandoned house.

Well, we don't really know if he died; maybe he wasn't even there when the house caught fire.

A friend who saw the fire told me that all the onlookers became frightened and ran away when they heard a loud scream and saw a huge ball of fire rising from the flames and climbing skyward until they could no longer see it.

(*Chele Chile, doubtful.*) Now that sounds like a mystery movie.

Well, that's what they told me.

8

Lina and the three children found Lencho and Calixto eating breakfast.

"They caught us with the tortilla in our hands!" said Lencho. "Come on, let's eat."

Calixto went to embrace his wife, then the children, lifting the smallest one in his arms. They greeted the old man, who always had kind words for them.

"We went around the block three times," said Lina, "to make sure no one was following us."

"Don't worry," said Lencho. "I don't think they'd come looking for you here."

"So many strange things happen nowadays," said Lina. "No one is safe anywhere."

"That's for sure," agreed Lencho.

"What worries me the most is working," said Calixto. "I can't stay hidden for long."

"You can't go back to your job anymore," said Lina.

"That's for sure," seconded Lencho.

"And where am I going to work then?"

"Anywhere except there."

"What a shame! It was so hard to get that job. The salary is miserable, but it's better than nothing."

"Toño's idea isn't a bad one," said Lencho.

"What idea is that?" inquired Lina.

"To try his luck in the United States," responded the old man.

"What?"

"Toño, Juancho's cousin, came by a while ago to say goodbye. He's going to Washington. His brother and some cousins live there."

"Yes, I remember them," said Lina. "A relative told me they're doing very well there."

"That's what Toño said too," agreed Lencho.

"How much money do you need for the trip?" asked Lina.

"The first part costs four hundred dollars," said Calixto sadly.

"And that's only part of the cost, for one person," said Lencho. "I imagine that for a couple with three children it would be much more."

"They say it's a long and dangerous trip," said Lina.

"But even so, it's not a bad idea," persisted Lencho.

"But there are five of us," said Calixto.

"You don't have to all go together either. Calixto is the one they're looking for. He can go first to try his luck and after he gets a job and gets to know the place, then the rest of you go," the old man advised. "What do you think?"

Lina and Calixto often sought Lencho's advice when they had problems, and the old man always helped them find a solution. And although he was now talking about something that was difficult for them to understand, especially at this desperate time, they trusted him completely, as they always had.

"But we don't have any money saved," said Lina. "We could never come up with that amount of money, not even in our dreams."

"You'll have to get it somehow," said Lencho. "It's the only way out. We can get the money together, even if it's one penny at a time."

"Maybe Hortensia could lend us something," said Calixto.

"I'll borrow money from everyone I know," offered the old man.

"Maybe it's not even worth it," said Lina doubtfully. "Maybe Calixto doesn't want to go."

"Who would want to leave his family to go to a strange country?" said Calixto. "No one, not even a crazy person. Unless you're in a desperate situation, like I am."

Lina hugged Calixto warmly, and said to him, "Like Lencho says, after you get there and start working and save some money, then we'll go. And we'll be together again."

"It's the only way," said Lencho.

"And where do we start?" asked Calixto.

"I'm going to try to borrow as much money as I can in the next couple of days," offered Lencho.

"I'm going back to Hortensia's," said Lina, "to see how much she can lend us."

"I'm going to visit some good friends," said Calixto. "I'm sure they can lend me some money."

"No, Calixto," begged Lencho. "It's too dangerous for you to go out."

"Yes, Calixto, you'd better stay here," urged Lina. "We'll take care of everything. I know we'll get the money somehow."

"But my God!" said Calixto. "To get that much money together, you have to borrow from a lot of people, and I can't just sit here waiting and biting my fingernails."

"Tonight we'll go visit José too," stated Lencho. "Maybe he can put us in touch with the *coyote* who's leaving next week."

That night Lencho and Calixto went to visit José, who resided in a small boardinghouse in a nearby neighborhood. They found him resting in a hammock outside his room. José recognized the old man immediately and got up to greet him. José was a young man, dark-skinned, of medium height with an easy, friendly smile.

"I want you to meet Calixto," said Lencho. "He's Macario's brother."

"Nice to meet you," said José. "You're Lina's husband, aren't you?"

"That's right," said Calixto. "And if I remember correctly, you're Menche's husband."

"Of course," said José, and then he shouted, "Menche, some friends are here!"

"Well I'm glad you know each other," said Lencho.

A woman emerged from the darkness of the room and greeted the visitors.

"Bring us some coffee," José requested of Menche.

"Yes of course," she said, inviting them to sit down. She left the room and returned a little later with the coffee.

"Well, your nephew Toño came to say goodbye this morning," said the old man. "He said he was going to the North."

"That's right," said José. "We were planning to leave together but I wasn't able to get the money on time, and he had to leave. I hope everything goes all right for him."

"Toño said you're going next week," said Lencho.

"Exactly. Tomorrow I'm going to get my passport and buy a suitcase and a pair of tennis shoes and take off to the Uniteds, as the Salvadorans who live over there say, to try my luck, because here things are going from bad to worse. It's been four months since I've had a permanent job. I work one day and am forced to rest the next three. It doesn't make sense. Sometimes we don't have anything to eat and the stores don't want to give us anything on credit anymore. We're on the brink of disaster. The only thing I haven't done is steal. I pray to God I never reach that extreme, because although I'm poor, I'm a decent person."

"Do you have children?" asked Calixto.

"Two," said José. "And Menche is three months pregnant. So in six months there'll be another mouth to feed in this family. But by then I hope to be working over there, in any kind of job, to support them even though I'll be far away."

"Well, Calixto wants to go too," remarked Lencho.

"Is he out of work too?" asked José.

"Well, yes," said Calixto. "I lost my job yesterday morning. I was working as a mason."

"What happened? Did they fire you? Or did the job just end?"

For a few seconds Calixto was silent, looking around with a nervous expression. Finally he said, "I was reported; they're accusing me of being an enemy of the government. Nothing but slander, because I'm not involved in anything political."

"Oh, I understand now," said José. "That's terrible!"

"The worst part is that Calixto doesn't get involved in any of those things," said Lencho. "I know for a fact that he's a working man interested only in the well-being of his family."

"Someone who was jealous of you must have reported you," said José. "That's common nowadays. If somebody doesn't like you for whatever reason, they report you to the authorities and, while the matter is being cleared up, you're in jail. Lucky they didn't arrest you."

"That's why I think it's best that I leave the country," said Calixto.

"The first thing is to find a good guide," said José. "And the most important thing is getting the money. Because without the money, forget it friend, you don't get anything. By pure luck I've managed to get the money to pay for the trip to Mexico, and once I'm there, my brother who lives in Washington is going to lend me the rest to pay for crossing the border."

"I think that in a week we can get the money together," declared Lencho. "We're going to look really hard."

"Well, if you want, I'll talk to the guide," offered José. "That way maybe we can go together, which would be better, because it's safer to travel with someone you know and trust."

"Please do that for me," asked Calixto. "I'll thank you with all my heart. I really need your help right now."

"No problem," said José. "Tomorrow you come with me; we'll talk to the man who arranges the trips and go get our passports too."

"It would make me really happy if you two went together," said Lencho. "Because they say that the trip is full of difficulties. You hear so many things. They say many people have been abandoned, lost in strange lands."

"A friend who made the trip and managed to cross the border just came back after working over there for three years," commented José. "He told me about the horrible things that happen on those trips. Everyone's afraid. The rumors are true! The *coyotes* abuse the women and rape them, they'll kill anyone for a few dollars, and they abandon women and children in the desert for no good reason. Many travelers have disappeared and never been heard from again. This friend says that, the farther you get on the trip, everything you've heard pales in comparison to what's really happening. The *coyotes* treat the people like animals. In Mexico, once you get past the capital, your life isn't worth anything."

"What a trip!" exclaimed Lencho.

9

(Kitchen. Calixto, Juancho.)

When the *migra* arrived at the hotel, everyone panicked.

Most of the employees escaped in the blink of an eye! I took off running.

Me too. The only one they caught was Caremacho.

They say that he was distracted, flirting with Pateyuca.

The waitress?

Yes.

What could Caremacho see in Pateyuca?

Rumor has it that he wanted to marry her just to get his green card.

What a user!

But it backfired on him because, while he was flirting with her, they trapped him in the kitchen and caught him.

Because of his own stupidity he was left with nothing.

And now the *migra* is going around checking all the restaurants and hotels in the area.

You have to be alert at all times.

But all the same, you have to work anyway you can, so you have to run the risk of being caught.

(Caremacho enters the kitchen. Calixto and Juancho are surprised.)

Hi, Caremacho! What are you doing here? I figured you were in jail!

We all thought you were locked up. Don't tell me you escaped!

No. They held me for five days. They were ready to deport me.

And how did you get out?

Someone paid the bond, so they let me go.

(Juancho, intrigued.) Who? You don't have any relatives in this country. Besides, they ask for a lot of money for those bonds.

A thousand dollars!

That's a lot of money.

And who paid it?

(Caremacho smiles.) My girlfriend.

Pateyuca?

Her name is Bettie.

Oh, Veri . . . *(Juancho struggles with the pronunciation.)*

No, it's not Veri. It's pronounced *beh-tee.*

Well anyway, that's wonderful. She lent you the money!

(Juancho winks at Caremacho.) She must really trust you.

She sure does. But I was really surprised when she came to pay the bond. I figured I was as good as gone.

And when are you going to pay her back? It's so much money!

She told me not to worry about it, to pay her when I can.

Wow, man, that sounds pretty serious! You're lucky to have found such an understanding person.

Yeah, really lucky. That woman saved my skin. She's not a bad person.

This is starting to smell like marriage.

If I were you, I'd propose to her.

I already did.

Well! Look how smart this Caremacho is, and here we were thinking he didn't have a clue!

Well, what did she say?

That we could get married whenever I wanted.

Don't waste time!

He's right.

I'm going to see if I can save some money. And then I'll marry her.

(Juancho hands him a beer.) This calls for a celebration!

It sure does! And if you need money, I can lend you a few dollars.

I can too. I have a little money put away that I'm saving to buy a used car, but I can lend it to you. But on one condition: you'd better invite us to the wedding!

Of course I'll invite you guys.

You can't forget your friends.

(*Caremacho, after a long drink of beer.*) Never. Good friends can never be forgotten.

10

The Immigration Office opened its doors at 8 a.m. By that time people were already waiting in a line that extended for several blocks. Many people would not get a chance to get their passports and, when the office closed for the day, would have no alternative but to wait in the same place until the next day.

Everyone came prepared for that eventuality. They brought with them food, folding chairs, blankets, and straw mats to sleep on, on the sidewalk, so they would not lose their place in line.

Calixto and José did not reach the door, and at five o'clock in the afternoon, when the Immigration Office closed, they were still about sixty people away.

"We'd better wait here until tomorrow," advised José. "If we move, when we get back we'll be so far away that we probably wouldn't get our passports tomorrow either."

"Fine," agreed Calixto. "I don't have anything to do anyway. I've got nothing to lose by sleeping out here in the street for one night. I'm sure we have worse things ahead of us."

"That's right," affirmed José.

At that moment a man approached them. "If you like, I'll hold your place while you run errands or eat. Don't worry; for only ten *colones* I'll keep it for you."

The man walked away when he realized that Calixto and José were not paying any attention to him.

"Just ignore him," the man behind them said. "Those guys just deceive you. They say they'll keep your place for you and when you walk away they sell it to someone else. So be careful."

"Thanks for the warning," José said. "Nowadays you can't trust anyone."

"Some will even fake fights or robberies," added the man. "Or they make something like a bomb go off, and when the people run away, they grab the best places in line, and later they sell them. This morning a couple of guys started fighting with knives, and they even drew blood, and when everyone ran out of line, their partners came up and took over the places of the people who had run. Then they sold the spots in line to the same people who had left them."

"I can't believe people even make a business out of the passport line," said Calixto.

"It's a matter of necessity," said José. "Everyone makes money any way they can, so they don't starve to death. It's the struggle to survive in the midst of misery."

A ragged, toothless old woman, accompanied by a dirty, skinny young boy, came and stood in front of Calixto. In a voice that sounded like a moan, she begged him, "Sir, please give me something, for the love of God."

José put a coin in the old woman's bony hand.

"Here, ma'am," he said to her. "Maybe you'll give me good luck on my trip."

"God bless you," said the elderly woman.

The man who, along with his wife, was in line in front of them, asked José, "Are you going to Guatemala?"

"Yes, but just passing through," answered José.

"Oh, really? And from there where are you going?"

"From there to Mexico," said Calixto. "And from there, if our luck holds, to the United States."

"That trip is *dangerous*," said the woman. "I wouldn't dare try it. A cousin of mine left on that trip three years ago and she was never heard from again. Our family doesn't know if she arrived safely, or got lost, or what happened to her."

"Maybe she found herself a *gringo* and got married," said the man jokingly, "and she doesn't want to have anything to do with her family anymore. Your cousin was very pretty."

To that the woman answered, "Aha, now I see! You liked my cousin better than me, didn't you?"

"No, my love," answered the man. "Never. Woman, there's no one else like you."

"Oh, well then," she said.

The man and woman hugged each other and began to talk about something else. Calixto and José renewed their own conversation.

Night had fallen, and the man behind them spread out a thin mattress on the ground and, before lying down, said, "Please wake me up if any trouble starts, or if the police come."

"Don't worry," said Calixto. "We'll keep watch."

José and Calixto continued talking quietly. An individual stopped and offered to buy their place in line, but when he saw they were ignoring him, he walked away.

"A friend who made the trip with my brother," said José, "had problems getting his passport. He didn't want to be identified."

"What did he do to get it?" asked Calixto, interested.

"The only way he could do it was by talking to certain people who supposedly find a way to get that type of document."

"False documents?"

"No, they're not fake. But this friend was afraid they'd identify him and arrest him right there. I don't know what kind of problems he had with the government."

"But couldn't he send someone else to get his passport?"

"No, he had to do it personally. He knew they wouldn't give it to anyone else."

"So how'd he finally work it out?"

"Well, he finally managed to see the contacts, but the problem was that he had to pay them a lot of money for getting him the papers without having to go through the required investigation."

"How much did he have to pay?"

"Five hundred *colones*."

"A month's pay!"

"That's right. But he had no alternative, so he paid and they got his passport for him, signatures, stamps and all."

"He must have had a good reason to be afraid that they'd recognize him."

"Yeah. Who knows what kind of mess he'd gotten himself into. The investigation they do is the way they detect people who are in trouble with the law."

"But money takes care of it."

"That's right."

"Was he your brother's friend?" asked Calixto.

"Yes, the same one who lent me the money to pay for my trip."

"He must have money."

"I really don't know. What I do know is that if he wouldn't have lent me the money, right now I'd still be running around trying to get it."

"He did you a big favor."

"Yeah, in exchange for another."

"What's that?"

"He lent me the money on the condition that I accompany and take care of his wife and his sister, who are going to travel with us."

"I see. You'll be their guardian."

"Exactly. And I promised him I'd protect them with my life."

"Are they pretty?" asked Calixto with a sly grin.

José smiled, and said, "Come on, Calixto, don't talk like that; what's not ours we don't touch."

"We can't touch but we can look," said Calixto.

Both of them burst out laughing.

11

JUDGE: Is your name Teresa?

INTERPRETER (*pointing*): No, it's her.

JUDGE: Are you Teresa?

TERESA: Yes, sir.

JUDGE: Do you speak and understand Spanish?

TERESA: Spanish, yes, but no English.

JUDGE: The interpreter, then, will translate from English to Spanish so that you will understand. Do you understand?

TERESA: No, not English.

JUDGE: Fine, the interpreter will translate into Spanish. Do you understand Spanish?

TERESA: Yes.

JUDGE: Very well. This is a deportation hearing. The law establishes that you are deportable because you entered this country without inspection and without legal documents. I'm going to determine if you should be deported or not. In this hearing you have the right to . . .

TERESA: What does "without inspection" mean?

JUDGE: Without what?

TERESA: Inspection.

JUDGE: You are being accused of sneaking across the border, without papers or permission.

TERESA: Yes, I . . . Yes, I entered without papers because they took them away from me.

JUDGE: Did you have a visa to enter the United States?

TERESA: No.

JUDGE: Where are your papers?

TERESA: Some men with big knives stole everything we had, our money too.

JUDGE: Where?

TERESA: In Tapachula.

JUDGE: Tapachula, is that in Mexico or Guatemala?

TERESA: Mexico.

JUDGE: When you arrived in this country, you had no papers. Is that correct?

TERESA: By then I didn't have them anymore.

JUDGE: Well, how did you enter if you didn't have papers?

TERESA: By sneaking across.

JUDGE: That is exactly what you are being accused of, of entering without papers, and that is what this hearing is about.

TERESA: What, Your Honor?

JUDGE: I'm going to determine if you entered without being inspected and properly admitted. Now, you have the right to be represented by a lawyer of your choice, but at no expense to the government. This means that if you want a lawyer, you have to make the arrangements. You should have received a list of organizations that have lawyers that might be willing to represent you free, as well as a paper describing your rights to appeal this hearing. Did you receive it?

TERESA: Yes.

JUDGE: Now, if you want the opportunity to speak with someone on the list of organizations or a private attorney to represent you in this hearing, I will continue your case while you make those arrangements. You may speak for yourself if you wish. If you wish to do so, I will permit that and we will go ahead with your hearing right now. What do you prefer? Do you need time to look for a lawyer or do you wish to speak for yourself?

TERESA: I don't understand the part about speaking for myself. What does that mean?

JUDGE: It means that if you want to go ahead with the hearing and answer the questions of the government's attorney, you may do so. But the law provides that if you wish to get a lawyer to represent you, you have the right to do that. Do you understand? Do you want an opportunity to get a lawyer?

TERESA: Yes.

JUDGE: Very well, now, was it your intention to apply for political asylum?

TERESA: Yes.

JUDGE: Is that what you want to do?

TERESA: Yes, I want political asylum.

JUDGE: I'm going to give you an application and you have ten days to fill it out, setting forth all the reasons you believe your life is in danger if you return to your country. Now, if you fill out the application and return it within ten days, the application will be processed. Afterward, in another hearing I will make a decision with regard to your application. But if you do not turn it in within ten days, a hearing will be scheduled for . . .

INTERPRETER: March 7, your Honor.

JUDGE: March 7?

INTERPRETER: Yes, at 10 a.m.

JUDGE: Very well, March 7 at 10 a.m. And if you wish to be represented by an attorney, he or she must be present with you on that date. Do you understand?

TERESA: Yes.

JUDGE: Now, you must be here for the hearing on March 7 at 10 a.m., unless you submit the application. Do you understand?

TERESA: Yes.

JUDGE: And if you submit your application, you will be given a new date for your hearing. But it you fail to submit your application within ten days, you must be here for the March 7 hearing, even if your bond is posted and you are released from INS custody. Do you understand?

TERESA: Yes.

JUDGE: And if you do not submit your application and if you do not appear for your hearing, I will make a decision in your case *in absentia*. Do you understand?

TERESA: Yes.

JUDGE: Don't forget. It's very important, and write down the date so you don't forget. Case continued.

12

They don't celebrate the Day of the Cross here.

What day is that?

May third.

How do they celebrate it in your country?

People put wooden crosses out in their yards and decorate them with colorful ribbons.

They hang all kinds of fruit from the crosses.

You kneel at the cross, say a prayer and take a piece of fruit. That's what I remember about that day.

I'll never forget May third. Since I was always hungry, I took advantage of that day to stuff myself with fruit.

While I was worshiping at the cross, saying the prayer, I'd be eyeing the biggest banana or mango. Then I'd snatch it up and take the first bite right there.

I'd go through the whole neighborhood. I'd kneel at each cross, cross myself, look quickly around to see if anyone was watching, and then put two pieces of fruit, sometimes three, into my bag.

You're only supposed to take one. To take two is a sin, Calixto.

I don't know if it's a sin. All I know is I had to take advantage of that day.

Didn't you get sick to your stomach from eating so much fruit?

I'd get indigestion and diarrhea. But I preferred that to going hungry.

It just so happened that I arrived in this country not long before May third. I remember I got up early that day so I could cover the whole neighborhood. The day before I had gone to the grocery store to get a big bag that I planned to fill with mangos and bananas.

You were really prepared, Juancho.

Man, I sure was; my mouth was watering just thinking about all the fruit I was going to eat.

And what did you think when you saw there were no crosses?

I was really disappointed. I got a bitter taste in my mouth. And I thought, "What a strange thing, they don't celebrate the Day of the Cross in this country."

They celebrate other things here. Like Thanksgiving.

And Halloween.

Once on the Day of the Cross, some friends took me to 14th Street, here in Washington, telling me that on that street people put out crosses with fruit on them like back home.

They played a joke on you, Calixto.

We went into a bar and suddenly I saw the pink body of a woman who was dancing on a stage while men were throwing money at her.

(*Loud laughter.*)

And what was your reaction?

I was shocked, and I said, "My God, that woman is naked!"

(*More laughter. Several waiters, hearing the laughs, enter the kitchen, among them Noé, a Cuban.*)

Come on, man, you'd never seen a naked woman? Unbelievable! What remote place do you come from?

Well in my town you don't see things like that. The women are so modest they don't take their clothes off in front of you even after you're married. Isn't that right, Juancho?

Go on! Before, in Havana, it was so common, man! There were places that had great shows—14th Street is nothing!

Well I couldn't believe what I was seeing.

So what did you do then?

I pinched myself to make sure I wasn't dreaming, because I had never seen bodies like that, not even in movies, much less in person.

I'll bet your mouth was hanging open.

And your eyes bugging out!

I was looking all around. I didn't understand why the other men didn't seem to be as excited as I was.

Did you go up close to the woman?

Yeah, and I got so carried away, I started making eyes at her. (*They laugh heartily.*)

And what did she do?

You guys aren't going to believe this, but she motioned to me that I should come closer.

She liked you!

That's what I thought too, and I got even more excited.

This Calixto is smooth with the ladies!

Well, I really believed that she liked me. And I got so nervous that I didn't know what to do when she was calling me to come closer.

The blonde made you freeze.

Until a friend explained to me that she was asking me for a dollar; then I held out a bill to her.

What happened then?

She couldn't reach it and motioned for me to come closer. But I couldn't take a step because I was so embarrassed.

The naked woman shook you up!

Then someone shoved me, and I crashed right into her. I felt my nose sinking between her huge breasts!

(*Loud laughter.*)

What a lucky nose you have, Calixto!

Then what happened?

Well, I was just dazed by the woman's pink body. So she took advantage of it and grabbed the dollar out of my hands and went off to the other side of the stage and never came back. I was kind of disappointed because for a minute I really thought she liked me.

Those gestures and smiles are just part of the business, Calixto.

I know. But when you're innocent, you can fall for that kind of woman, especially when they smile and move those great bodies of theirs.

You were kidding yourself.

When we left the bar it was dark, and outside some young, pretty women started walking with us: black ones, Asian ones and white ones, giving us all kinds of looks that gave me goose bumps and took my breath away.

Could you understand what they were saying?

One of the guys we were with explained that the women were saying that they'd go with us for money.

What did you guys do? Did you take them up on it?

No. We were just out for a walk.

Looking for crosses with fruit.

And there were no crosses, but there were women!

But there was fruit–enormous melons!

(*Roars of laughter.*)

But you can't grab them just by crossing yourself; you have to buy them with dollars!

So what do you think of 14th Street now?

Everything is just the opposite here. Back home not even Juana Mechuda would pay any attention to me, not even as a joke.

And who is Juana Mechuda?

A deaf-mute who used to wander around town throwing stones at people. She hit me once.

What a great girlfriend, Calixto. And you were keeping it a secret!

(*Laughter.*)

What I'm trying to say is that in my town, no matter how ugly or pretty the women are, they're hard to get. But here, on 14th Street, the women try to get us!

It's all for money, Calixto. Just for money.

13

On Monday morning, Calixto and José took a taxi and went to pick up Silvia and Elisa, the wife and sister of José's friend. They were waiting at the door, and got into the car. José told the driver to take them to Mejicanos, a large, sprawling, working-class neighborhood on the outskirts of San Salvador. They got out at the market and, since none of them were familiar with the neighborhood, they walked around lost for half an hour, until they finally found the place where the guide had told them to meet. The man had told José, "The day after tomorrow you will come to this address . . ."

José asked him, "And then what? Do I knock on the door?"

"The door will be open. Go in. It's a house with a yard like a peasant farmer's house."

"What time should we be there?"

"Between eleven in the morning and one in the afternoon."

The "house" turned out to be a shelter held up by six roughly cut tree trunks. The man had told him, "The door will be open," but the place had no doors. As they approached they saw several empty benches and others that were occupied by women, men, and some children.

Calixto got the impression that they were the last to arrive. The people were completely silent. The women all had their hands busy with something. The men were smoking. One walked nervously a few yards from the shelter.

José inspected the group with a quick glance. He noticed a young girl and wondered to himself, "Is she alone? Is she travelling with someone?"

The people appeared uneasy; they looked at each other impatiently. They were waiting for the guide but he had not arrived. Time passed and no one dared say a word. Three hours passed.

José thought, "I hope they didn't lie to us."

By now Calixto was sure they had been the last to arrive, and it seemed strange to him that in the lapse of three hours no one had spoken, so finally he tossed a question into the air: "Do you know Miguel?"

And that was the spark they needed, because from then on everyone talked.

"Where are you from?"

"Do you have children you're leaving behind?"

"Where are you going?"

They also began to share what little they carried and to take papers out of their bags. They looked like they were in uniform. Each of them carried a small suitcase and wore blue, gray, or black clothing, and tennis shoes. There were thirty of them altogether, and Calixto noticed several children. He thought that the youngest might be about seven years old, and the child reminded him of one of his own.

Finally someone arrived, but no one paid any attention because at that moment they seemed possessed by the fever of showing each other what they had brought with them. An elderly man was showing the inside compartment of his belt where he had hidden the address and telephone number of the place he was going. Suddenly he became panic-stricken, fearful of getting lost or that the information he had was wrong. Then, he set about the task of writing down other people's addresses. This desperation was contagious; the others also began to exchange information.

"And you, where are you going? Give me the phone number, just in case."

"Yes, take down the number; the lady is a very nice person. She's a fat little lady who walks like this, you see, and lives in a white house."

"In Los Angeles?"

"Yes, in Los Angeles, near a store."

They were all trying to find something they did not have at that moment. Their only possessions were the clothes they were wearing and a bag that barely held their personal hygiene items and one

change of clothes. They had left behind all their material and senti-
mental possessions, however many or however few those may have
been. The telephone numbers and addresses represented for them
points of reference in the new world to which they were heading, a
base of support in a strange place, a small hope. But when the guide
saw the exchange that was taking place, he scolded them immediately: "No, no. Keep things to yourselves, because the *migra* might
arrest those people, go to those houses and find other undocumented people because of papers that they take away from you. There's
no reason to put them at risk too."

José looked at the guide and the first thing he noticed was his
toothless smile. He had one arm in a cast, maybe broken in a fight. In
addition, he looked like a drunk.

Then his deputy arrived, a man who looked like a foreigner to
Calixto and the others. He wore a cowboy hat, fine leather boots, and
a tight-fitting fringed jacket. The one with the broken arm was of simple appearance, open conversation and quite kind to the travelers.

The smugglers looked over the group and with crude, indiscreet
stares examined the young women, who turned toward their companions to make clear that they were not traveling alone. No one
complained or said anything.

"Do you all have the money?" asked the one with the broken arm.

"Yes!" the men and women answered.

"Very good," he said. "Because you know that without the money
no one goes anywhere."

"And, to start, I need a hundred dollars from each of you. So, let's
have it!"

Everyone got out their money.

"But we want dollars," said the other smuggler. "Nothing but dollars. *Colones* aren't worth anything here."

After collecting the first payment from everyone in the group,
one of the guides said, "Before we leave, we'll tell you some things
you must remember for the whole trip."

"We're going to teach you how to protect yourselves in Mexico,"
added the other. "And to avoid saying certain words that would give
you away."

"What I'm telling you is that you have to start thinking like Mexicans. Okay?"

The group remained silent, listening intently, but suddenly it occurred to José to say, "The only Mexican thing I know are *ranchera* songs."

Nervous laughter and a few comments were heard.

"That's okay," said the guide. "Who knows? Those *rancheras* may come in real handy."

"Have you all seen Mexican movies?" asked one of the guides.

"Yes," some of them answered.

"Well, from now on you have to talk with that accent, that sing-song voice Mexicans speak with."

"There are some Salvadoran words you should never say. For example, don't say *pisto* when you're talking about money."

"You also have to know the date of Mexico's Independence Day," the National Anthem and the history of Mexico in general. We'll be teaching you all this during the trip, and you need to remember it."

"When we're in Mexico, if they ask you where you're from, you should say 'I'm from Guanajuato.'"

"And if they ask you what Guanajuato is like, you just say that in the center of town there's a very tall tower."

One of the smugglers began to divide them into small groups: "You're going to be from León, Guanajuato; you're from Jalisco; you're from Guerrero; and you're going to be from Mérida, Yucatán."

"There's a place in the Yucatán that's close to Guatemala where they talk something like Salvadorans do. But I don't advise you to say you're from there because the Mexican *migra* already knows that and they're going to suspect you're lying. If they stop you in Ciudad Juárez, better say you're from there."

"Then they're going to ask you if you've been to such-and-such a bar, and they're going to catch you because maybe the bar they name doesn't even exist. The most famous bars in Ciudad Juárez are El Charro de la Frontera, La Princesa del Norte, and La Cantinita. So memorize those names."

"Well, that's all for today. Later we'll teach you other things that will help you on the trip. Things that could save your lives. But now we're going to check your clothing and luggage."

Calixto got the feeling that the men were carefully checking the contents of their luggage with the sole intention of seeing what each one held.

One woman seemed a little reticent to open her bag, but the guide insisted and she was forced to do so.

"And that gold you have there? Who's it for?" asked the man with obvious interest.

"It's for some relatives who live in Los Angeles," she said. "They asked me to bring it."

The two guides exchanged glances, and one of them smiled wickedly.

"The clothes you're wearing are too bright," one of them said to a woman who was wearing an ocher-colored blouse. "Don't you have another outfit?"

"Yes," answered the man who accompanied her. "She has some dark clothes."

"Okay, then change your clothes the first chance you have. Are you traveling with her?"

"Yes," answered the young man.

"Are you married?"

"Yes."

One of the guides approached a young woman who appeared to be traveling alone and, after examining the bulging contents of her bag, said, "You're bringing too many clothes. See if anyone else has room in their suitcase to help you carry some of this; otherwise you'll have to leave it. Remember, this isn't a vacation."

"Well," said the other, "then we're ready to leave. Now we're going to divide you into groups."

"From now on these groups will always stay together, until we reach the border."

"Those who have no documents come over here," ordered the man with the cast on his arm.

Seven people stepped to his side.

"You will be a special group that at certain times will separate from the rest of us and take a different route. You can't go the whole way with the rest because we're going to go through customs and you have to show your papers there."

Following the orders of the guides, the travelers abandoned the shelter and went out into the street. Awaiting them there were several rental cars which took them to the bus terminal, where they boarded a big, comfortable bus, the kind usually used by tourists.

At about six o'clock in the afternoon they arrived at the Guatemalan border. They got out of the bus and entered the customs office for the routine inspection. They had already been warned that at customs they would have to pay a certain amount of money and that they should have it ready.

Calixto followed the example of the others, opened his bag and deposited its contents on the table. The customs agent, after a cursory examination and with no explanation took Calixto's deodorant and put it into a drawer.

"I don't know why he took it," thought Calixto. "Maybe his armpits stink, he needs deodorant, and he liked mine."

Calixto decided to keep quiet about it and not complain.

While some of the agents were examining the luggage, others had taken the travelers' documents and seemed to be checking lists, as if looking for someone in particular. They glanced quickly at the travelers and Calixto felt chills when he realized that one of the inspectors was staring at him. He pretended not to notice, but feared they would take him aside to interrogate him and make him confess that he was being looked for in his country for political reasons. Then they would surely arrest him and turn him over to the authorities of his country. But a few seconds later, Calixto saw that the man lit a cigarette and was smoking. Calixto decided that all of them were mainly concerned with what they could confiscate.

José, on the other hand, was wondering if the inspectors had guessed the purpose of the trip and concluded that it was impossible for them not to know, since everyone in the group carried small suitcases, wore dark clothing, all the men wore tennis shoes and the women flats. They were going to Guatemala, yet they had virtually no luggage.

"You can tell a mile away that our intent is to enter the United States illegally," he thought. "It's written all over us. Now I understand why we have to pay a bribe so they don't give us a hard time."

José was right; the group was marked. And their intentions would become even more obvious as they got closer to Mexico City, or went around it, whichever route the astute guides decided the odyssey should take.

When the bus resumed its journey after going through customs, Calixto leaned back in his seat and closed his eyes to rest, trying to escape from what was happening around him. He heard the bus driver say, "We're in another country now," and he was suddenly overwhelmed by reality. He was leaving his homeland, something he had not been fully conscious of until that moment. During the scramble to get the money to pay for the trip, he had thought of nothing else. But now the full realization that he was leaving hit him, and he felt a profound nostalgia for his people and his home and, to console himself, he began to remember everything he could with great passion and detail, as if his very existence depended on that memory. With his eyes closed, he traveled mentally through his neighborhood, reconstructing it. The images came to life and paraded through his memory, becoming his sole consolation. Although he was physically moving away from his land, he firmly believed that he would always hold it in his heart.

14

RESIDENCE IN THE PARK

When night fell on the city, Armando entered Central Park—located in the heart of Manhattan between 59th and 110th Streets—in search of a place to sleep. After so long, it was like home to him and he was familiar with the surroundings, the least dirty sectors, and had even learned to see in the dark, "like a bat," he thought.

About 30 homeless people of different origins, speaking diverse languages—Latinos, Asians and even Americans—regularly spent the night in that wooded park. Those nocturnal inhabitants represented something like the "United Nations of Misfortune," headquartered in the park, so unlike the United Nations, the international entity located in a beautiful skyscraper between 42nd and 48th Streets along the bank of the East River, not very far from there, made up of important representatives from all the countries of the world.

Armando improvised a bed out of cardboard and leaves, lay down carefully and closed his eyes. Accompanied by a serenade of crickets and the strange noises of nocturnal animals, he thought about the loved ones he had left behind. From time to time he opened his eyes to scrutinize his surroundings and make sure that no other vagabond, or thief, was preparing to ambush him, since it was common for the members of the group to commit assaults on each other. One night he had been violently awakened by a group of beggars who, armed with clubs and stones, forced him to turn over the last three dollars he had. Life was cruel in that underworld, and one could not trust even his own companions in misery.

But more than his personal situation, he was concerned about his family. He needed to make money and send it to them because they were dependent upon him for support. Back home they believed he was doing fine, "swimming in a sea of money." They had no idea that he lived in the street and suffered the rigors of cold and hunger. They would never believe it. They would say, "How is it possible that there are homeless people in the richest nation on earth?" But of course there were; he was a living, irrefutable example. "If not, let them see how I dress, where I sleep and what I eat," he thought sadly.

More than once the desperate nature of his circumstances had made Armando think about stealing, but his grandmother's advice persisted in his memory: "Son, a decent person should never steal."

Armando's only desire was to get a permanent job, something he had not attained in spite of having arrived in the United States twelve months before with the dream of buying a convertible, getting rich and sending money to his family so they could join him. In his country, his bus driver's salary had not been sufficient to provide his wife and children with a decent existence. There was no future in that occupation; the salary was miserable and on top of that the owners of the buses accused the drivers of stealing the fares.

Armando borrowed money and paid a *coyote*. After a long, arduous journey by bus, train and on foot through El Salvador, Guatemala and Mexico, and finally in a gasoline tank-truck suited for the traffic of undocumented people, he crossed the U.S. border and went to seek his fortune in the big city of New York. Supposedly a friend awaited him there, but unbeknownst to Armando, just a week before, the friend had been captured by Immigration and deported to his country. Julio, a Mexican who then lived in the friend's room, befriended Armando, gave him a place to stay and introduced him to the Latino *barrio* of Manhattan.

At first Armando worked in a restaurant, washing dishes; later he got a construction job and rented a room. Eventually the opportunities became scarce and the ranks of the unemployed swelled. He was unable to pay rent, after being out of work for several weeks, and was evicted.

Like many homeless people, Armando did not have a work permit from the Immigration and Naturalization Service, nor the right to benefits of federal welfare programs, which many of the undocumented avoided for fear of being deported. For the same reason they hesitated to spend the night in homeless shelters; they feared being required to present papers and being reported to Immigration.

Lying among the bushes, Armando told Julio about a memorable meal: "It was my first full meal since I came to this country: french fries, chicken and apple pie. But now I don't even have a dollar for a piece of bread."

Julio, who had been a teacher in Mexico, was so affected by going hungry that he became ill: "Several times I've gone as much as three days without eating anything at all, and I've felt that my head was spinning."

Armando added, "When they see us looking like this, they label us delinquents, but we're decent people like anyone else. We're homeless and hungry only because we're unemployed."

"It's not our fault either," declared Julio. "We make so many sacrifices to get to this country, truly desiring to get ahead, and we just have bad luck. But we don't lose hope. Who knows, maybe one of these days we'll find a job."

"That's reality," agreed Armando. "People insult us and scream at us to go back to our country."

"I'd rather die than go back like this," said Julio. "My family and friends would never forgive me. They'd say I had the opportunity in my hands and didn't know how to take advantage of it."

Armando added, "After the war my country was left in poverty, and unemployment went up, forcing a lot of people to steal. Meanwhile, here I am trapped in this strange situation. But it's best for us to stay here any way we can; that way we lessen the problems in our countries. Like they say back home: One less Indian, one more tortilla."

> *La Crónica del Barrio*
> New York
> April 5, 1995

15

JUDGE: Are you Teresa?

TERESA: Yes.

JUDGE: Do you speak and understand Spanish?

TERESA: Yes.

JUDGE: All right, I continued this case in February to give you an opportunity to apply for political asylum, but you have not submitted an application.

TERESA: But the man from the church just came to fill out the form yesterday.

JUDGE: Is he going to fill it out for you?

TERESA: Yes, he already did and . . .

JUDGE: All right.

TERESA: And he brought it here yesterday.

JUDGE: Fine, then you will have ten days from today to submit it. Do you understand? And if you don't submit it within the next ten days, I won't give you any more time, and you must be here for a hearing on April 1 at two o'clock in the afternoon. Do you understand?

TERESA: What time?

JUDGE: 2 p.m.

TERESA: Two o'clock in the afternoon?

JUDGE: Do you understand that?

TERESA: Yes . . . But the man from the church took the paper and he said he was going to send it.

JUDGE: Fine, but make sure he submits it within ten days; otherwise I will have to reject your application. Do you understand?

TERESA: Yes.

JUDGE: Very well. Now, if you do not submit the application, you must be here for a hearing on April 1 at two o'clock in the afternoon. Do you understand?

TERESA: Yes.

JUDGE: Case continued.

16

A large, faded sign proclaimed, "The Pearl of the South." José pushed the dark swinging doors, and they emitted a creaking sound, like a moan. Once inside, he had the sensation of being in a warm, dark cave in whose interior he discovered several customers who at first were shadows but within seconds took on the shapes of strange, mummified beings. One of the figures, which resembled a woman, occupied the table in a corner next to the bar. She was drinking alone from an empty glass; she got up and, with slow, staggering steps, came to greet him.

"Not even the hookers look good here," José thought to himself, watching her as she approached.

He sat down. A rancid stench came from the bathroom.

The walls of the place, cracked and of indefinite color, were covered with several framed pictures, some under glass and others simply nailed to the wall. Most notable among them was the voluptuous figure of a naked woman with long, dark hair, reclining in a suggestive pose. On another wall was the image of the Sacred Heart of Jesus surrounded by saints. Next to it was an expired calendar. Near the grouping, a saying was written on the wall declaring, "Life is a gamble."

In the bathroom someone began to vomit with such noise and force that it sounded like he was throwing up his guts. José moved to a different table.

"The Pearl of the South," he thought. "What a name. This place seems more like the sewer of the south."

The woman approached, not saying a word. She remained there motionless, like a mummy.

"A beer," José said, as if to scare her away.

She made a strange gesture and slowly turned her back, heading toward the bar.

"At this rate she'll bring me my beer tomorrow."

A man emerged from the bathroom and, bumping into tables and chairs all the way, finally arrived at the jukebox and made several selections. The despondent *ranchera* song seemed to console him. He went to sit with two men who occupied a table and from there, through uncontrollable belching, yelled "Celina, three more beers!"

"Come on, don't drink so much," said one of his companions. "Remember we have to get up early tomorrow to continue our trip. The people are impatient to leave."

"They've already waited three days," said the drunken one. "They can wait one more."

"How many are you taking?" asked someone from another group.
"Twenty-five."

"That's a good-sized group. Where are you planning to cross?"
"Tijuana."

"Be careful. That place is being watched more than usual. Our last trip we had thirty people and they were all caught. We were lucky to get away."

The woman gave the men their drinks and brought two beers to José. She sat down next to him and said, "I thought you might buy me a beer; that's why I brought two."

"That's fine," said José, pushing the bottle toward her.

"Headed north?"

"Yes, hoping to find a good job."

"That's where I was going too," she said. "And I can't explain how I ended up staying in this damn town."

"Why didn't you go back to your country?"

"Because staying here is better than going back to misery."

José ordered two more beers and, while he waited for her to return, went to the bathroom, where he poured out the contents of the bottle, returning to the table with the empty container.

"A lot like you pass through here," said the woman when she returned with the drinks. "With big dreams. Some are convinced they'll become millionaires over there."

"The hope of a better life pushes you to leave your family and country," commented José.

The voice of Miguel Aceves Mejía came from the jukebox:

> I'm in the corner of a bar
> listening to my song,
> they're serving me my tequila
> and my thoughts turn to you . . .

A customer joined in with the song. Another gave a shout that sounded like a howl.

"Those *coyotes* are already crazy from too many drinks," said the woman. "They're all alike. They forget about the people. They keep them locked up and make them go hungry just to get drunk."

"Is that how they treat the travelers?"

"That's the least of it! They treat them like animals."

"So you were going to the North too?"

"Yeah . . . with a lot of dreams. But one of the guides and I fell in love, and when we got here we spent three days and nights making love like newlyweds. When it was time to continue the trip, he convinced me that I should stay here because it was too dangerous. He delayed the trip two more days. When he left he gave me a lot of money and begged me to wait for him. When he came back we were going to get married . . . I remember his last words: 'You're the woman I've searched for all my life. We'll get married and be happy. I'll treat you like a queen.'"

"Celina, three more beers!" The shouts interrupted the woman's story.

"Four more for me," said José.

"This guy drinks like a fish," she thought as she got up. She did not realize that José would take a couple of drinks from the bottle and then go to the bathroom and pour out the rest. It was part of his strategy for confronting the guides, if they came to the bar, those heartless men capable of anything in that desolate, lawless border town.

They had left their country behind and stopped at that remote Guatemalan border town called Tecún Umán, where they were staying at a guest house, a big old building divided into small bedrooms, designed specifically for the traffic of undocumented persons. At that time the group consisted of thirty people. After having a light supper they went to their assigned rooms, where they slept the first night of the journey.

While they were resting, Silvia commented to José that one of the guides had acted extremely vulgar and pushy toward her.

"He's been asking me who you really are, and if we're really married."

"Don't worry," José had replied. "From now on we'll never split up and I'll keep a close eye on their moves."

The next morning Silvia decided to take a shower and, while the water was running, one of the smugglers tried to force open the door. José intervened immediately: "What's wrong with you? Where do you think you're going? Can't you see there's someone in the bathroom?"

"Look, don't tell me your stories. She's not your wife and the other one isn't your sister."

The man walked away. José returned to the room and told Calixto what had happened.

"It's not going to be easy to get him to leave Silvia alone," said Calixto, "and that's a real problem. We're in their hands and can't make enemies of them because they could get back at us by leaving us abandoned in the middle of nowhere."

"But somehow we have to show him that we won't let him push us around."

"I don't think words will be enough to convince him."

"That's for sure. He'll only understand if we do it his way."

"Be careful," warned Calixto. "These guys are a thousand times sneakier than we are."

After meditating about the problem all day. José asked Calixto to take care of the women, and he went out to walk around. About four o'clock in the afternoon he found a store.

He entered and asked, "Do you sell knives?"

The shopkeeper looked at him curiously for a moment as José, unruffled, stood silently in the middle of the store. The man nodded slowly.

"I need a medium-sized one, well-sharpened."

At five o'clock José returned to the room. The guides were chatting with the owner of the place out in the hall. Knowing they would hear him, José almost shouted, saying to Calixto, "I'm going to go for a walk!"

"Where?" asked Calixto.

"The Pearl of the South is just two blocks from here. I'll be there, having a beer."

The jukebox began playing a new song. The melancholy voice of Julio Jaramillo filled the darkness of the bar:

> I'm lonely without you
> and can't forget you
> not even for a moment,
> I live without love
> waiting for someone
> who doesn't love me . . .

The woman returned with two beers in each hand. José asked, "And what happened to your boyfriend?"

She sighed and said, "God only knows. He never came back, and I was left here waiting for him. I believed our love would last a lifetime, but fate wasn't on our side."

> I see time going by
> and winter arrives
> everything but you . . .

The other customers ordered more beer, and the woman went to wait on them. At that moment the doors swung open abruptly, revealing the faint light of sundown. José saw the smugglers come in; they headed right for him. Seeing the number of empty bottles on the table, they were sure he was drunk. José put one hand under the table, readied the sharp knife and held it tightly.

One of the guides said, "Look, cut the shit. The deal is I like those women. I like them."

The other one threw a wad of bills onto the table.

"We'll give you two hundred for each of them. You can't lose. You lose absolutely nothing. I even like you as a friend, and I won't charge you for taking you across the border. Take the money."

José glared at him scornfully. "Those women aren't for sale. No deal."

"Stop jerking us around. Don't be a fool. What's it to you if we go to bed with them? After all, they're nothing to you."

José made a quick move, and before the man could back up he put the tip of the shiny knife to his throat and said, "I said no, and if you push it, *this* is the only deal we'll make. So you decide."

The smuggler laughed loudly, not out of fear, but mockingly. José withdrew the knife for a second, and then put it back to the man's throat: "Laugh at me if you want, but I make no deals."

The man laughed again, "I definitely like you. Let's forget about the women and have a beer."

José put the knife away, but did not let his guard down. The other man shouted, "Bartender, three beers! One for me and one for each of my friends!"

The three men raised the bottles and drank. The jukebox sang with the strong voice of Vicente Fernández:

> No longer can I follow you
> your path is longer than mine
> you go in search of other arms
> My fate is to remain behind . . .

17

(Kitchen. Calixto, Cali, Juancho, Chele Chile)

Fate plays with us. I never imagined that one day I would be washing dishes in a foreign land. In my country I did everything; I began as a day laborer in my village, and after I went to the capital, I worked as a shoemaker and then as a mason. That is, when I wasn't on a binge, because the desperation of unemployment and misery pushes you to alcoholism. But here in this country I'm like a new man, I rarely drink and I work in a kitchen, a job usually reserved for women in our country.

So in a way, you've made progress, Calixto.

So it seems.

I never imagined either that after herding cows back home, I'd be so far away, living in such a different place.

What's the name of the town you come from?

Ojo de Agua.

Is it big?

No, it's just a tiny village on a mountain full of snakes and iguanas.

It's not that bad; I bet it's a pretty little town.

It was. But there were battles there between the guerrillas and the army. The bombs destroyed the place and those of us who survived fled to other cities. Now it's a ghost town.

I can see you really miss your country.

Why wouldn't I? I was born and raised there, and learned such important things.

Like what? What can you learn in a place as far from civilization as that?

Well, to use a machete.

And herd oxen and cows.

To ride a horse.

And plant crops.

Harvest cotton.

And hunt iguanas.

Drink moonshine.

And chew tobacco.

All the things a man has to learn in order to survive in the country. Even to respect the authorities.

What do the authorities do out in the country?

They chase down kidnappers.

And put people who sell moonshine in jail.

(*Chele Chile to Caremacho.*) And how do you know? I thought you were from the capital.

I am from the capital. But I know what country life is like.

In the country you work really hard. It's not a life for wimps.

That's for sure. I used to get up real early in the morning, long before the sun came up. My breakfast was a couple of tortillas with beans and cheap coffee.

Why did you get up so early?

Because I used to walk as much as five kilometers to get to the hacienda where I picked cotton.

Five kilometers just to get there?

That was nothing. In the country everyone walks everywhere.

On the hacienda I'd work from sunup 'til sundown, for a few *colones* and a couple of tortillas with salt every day, and with cruel crew leaders as bosses.

The owners of the hacienda?

No, the crew leaders are poor peasants like the rest of the workers. But they think they're powerful and end up even meaner than the owners themselves.

They treat their own people terribly, lie to the bosses about them so they fire them or don't pay them the salary they should.

A poor man with a little power at times can become more cruel than a rich man. The rich use the poor to repress the poor.

After work I felt dead tired and starved. But even so, I had to walk the five kilometers back home.

A lot of the workers slept at the hacienda.

I could have done that. But I preferred to go home every day because I missed my wife and children.

It was dangerous at night on the hacienda. There were brawls when the workers got drunk; they would fight with machetes, wounding or even killing each other. The crew leaders would take advantage of the darkness of night to rape the girls. And no one could say anything or they'd be reported to the authorities. They say that there are a lot of virgins at the beginning of the cotton harvest, but not one when it ends.

In the winter things were more difficult. It would rain so hard that the drops hitting your face felt like stones and almost beat your eyes out.

When I would get caught in a storm on the way home, I'd take cover in a cave.

I did that once, but a snake bit me on the arm.

Son of a . . .

I felt like I had been stabbed in the heart.

What did you do?

I sucked the blood out of the bite and spit it out. Then I took off my shirt and tied it around my arm so that the poison that had gotten into my blood wouldn't circulate through the rest of my body; otherwise I'd have died right there.

And who taught you all that?

It's one of the many things my father taught me from the time I was very small. Those are the things you learn in the country. Matters of life and death.

But then what happened?

I took off running, slipping and sliding in the mud in the midst of the thunderstorm. I felt like I was going to faint and fall into the mud. When I got home I fell over, head first, like a wounded animal. My wife and children dragged me into the house. I got such a high fever that I was sweating like crazy. I was delirious and talking nonsense. My wife stayed up all night, putting cold cloths on my forehead.

I'll bet you couldn't go to work the next day.

When I woke up in the morning, I felt so weak I could barely stand up. But I was so stubborn that I insisted I was going to work and asked my wife to serve me breakfast.

If I were you, I wouldn't have gone—not in that condition.

But we needed the money. So after eating breakfast I put a wad of tobacco in my mouth and started on the long walk to the hacienda, down the valley, the first rays of the morning sun shining on me, with no desire other than to work.

Did you make it there?

Are you kidding? I had walked about five minutes when I fainted right there on the path.

You were dead.

My wife had figured that would happen. But being the good wife that she is, she didn't want to argue with me; she just followed me without my knowing it. Like all peasant women, in spite of being nourished only by beans, tortillas and salt, she's strong, of character and of body. She helped me up and carried me, dragged me, to the house.

So you slept that day.

How long before you went back to work?

For three days I was in bed, delirious and hallucinating because of the fever, with no medicine other than my wife's and children's tears and prayers.

Three days?

Yeah, three days that I didn't go to work and didn't make a dime.

Just imagine. Three days that the world didn't give a damn that a poor devil like Calixto was dying, abandoned in a poor shack, and that it would have made no difference if he did, because like they say back home. "Salvadorans are cheap and there are plenty of them."

(*Calixto sighs.*) My country is a difficult memory, because on the one hand it's the memory of hunger and misery, but on the other it's the beautiful memory of my people and my customs.

18

The next night the travelers continued their trip through Guatemala toward Mexico.

"We'll travel at night to avoid being detected," their leader had said.

It was a foggy night. The bus was moving slowly, its strong lights inadequate as they bounced off the solid wall formed by the thick fog, through which they could see absolutely nothing. The monotonous rumble of the engine was the only thing that disturbed the nocturnal silence of the jungle.

Suddenly the night air was pierced by intermittent rays of red light which seemed to strike the bus and the fog. The driver brought the vehicle to a stop. Everything and everyone remained in silence and suspense for about five minutes. No one spoke. The headlights and motor of the bus seemed to be the only signs of life.

Fierce-looking men carrying machine guns began to emerge from the thick mist; they quickly surrounded the vehicle. One of them pounded on the door, then made a sudden motion and shouted, "All the men out of the bus!"

The passengers got out and, following the man's orders, put their hands up. The men began to search them. They checked lists of names and photographs, exchanging words and gestures among themselves.

After thoroughly inspecting the passengers and comparing their faces with the photographs, all of which took about half an hour, they did not find the person they were looking for, and ordered everyone back to the bus.

They showed order and discipline. A short distance from the bus, one of them spoke with the guide, who, after a brief conversation, handed the armed man something, possibly money. The guide returned to the vehicle and the journey continued.

This happened two more times that same night. One of the smugglers always got off, stepped aside with one of the armed men and gave him something, perhaps payment for the right of passage over that foggy highway in the Guatemalan jungle.

Finally they crossed the border and entered Mexican territory.

At about nine o'clock in the morning, the bus stopped in a small town. Before getting out, one of the guides recommended, "We're going to stop at this market; you'd better get something to eat. But remember what we told you; you have to talk like Mexicans."

"When you're talking to each other, make sure to call each other *tú*, not *vos*," added the other. "And don't forget to speak with that sing-song accent that Mexicans have."

"Be very careful with everything you say. If they ask you if you have any *pisto*, just say no, because here *pisto* doesn't mean money, it means a shot of booze. Because if they ask you if you have any and you say 'Yes, here it is,' it could turn out that it's the *migra*, and they'll catch you right there. Understand?"

"Yes," they all responded.

"Okay, then get out and go eat. But don't wander too far because you might get lost and we'll leave you behind."

They got off the bus and followed the guides who, very sure of themselves, sat down on the benches of the open-air restaurant and ordered food.

"Ma'am, bring us some tacos, okay? And coffee."

Some of the passengers sat down with the guides and others went to separate tables.

Calixto and José, Silvia and Elisa had sat down at a table and, driven more by hunger than courage, José ordered tacos and coffee for the four of them. Unable to contain his laughter, he whispered, "This is really funny. I never imagined that one day, to get something to eat, I'd have to talk like a Mexican."

"It's not easy," said Elisa. "It's impossible to change your identity overnight."

At the next table, José noticed a group of fellow travelers, a couple with two children who were looking at each other fearfully, not daring to order food. José went over to them and asked, "Would you like me to order you some tacos?"

"Yes, please," begged the woman. "We're very hungry, but we can't talk like Mexicans; we're afraid we'll give ourselves away."

"Don't worry," said José.

He asked one of the cooks to serve some tacos, soft drinks and coffee to the family. They devoured it in a couple of minutes and then looked over at José with grateful expressions.

"I don't have the slightest idea where we are," said Calixto.

"Only the *coyotes* know," said Silvia. "We're completely in their hands."

"Yeah, they have their routes planned," said José, "but the important thing is we're already in Mexico."

"That's right," said Calixto. "We've been on the road for two days already."

"And that's nothing," said José. "It's still a long way to the U.S. border."

Calixto noticed that one of the guides was getting on the bus, followed by several passengers.

"It's time to get going," he said to the group.

The four of them got up and went to get on the bus. When everyone had gotten on, the bus pulled away from the market to continue its journey through small towns, whose names Calixto and José tried to pronounce, at times unsuccessfully. This provided them with a little distraction, because that part of the trip through the vast territory of Mexico was long, monotonous and tiring.

19

Spring had returned to Washington. Nature was finally awakening from the long lethargy of winter and displaying her splendor of flowers, colors and birds, filling the air with an ancient but refreshing message of renovation and hope.

That hot May afternoon, Calixto was at a small park located at the intersection of Mount Pleasant and Lamont Streets. He was chatting with Daniel, one of so many compatriots he had met in the neighborhood, and other friends who were enthusiastically sharing jokes and laughs, enjoying the nice weather and a break from their hard work. They were talking about their current situation, the state of affairs in their native land, and anything else that occurred to the group of friends who met every Sunday in that small park in Adams Morgan, the neighborhood inhabited by a large number of immigrants from El Salvador, who constituted the majority of the Latino population of Washington, D.C.

Two policewomen making their rounds in the neighborhood stopped in front of the group. One of them warned them that drinking alcoholic beverages in public parks was prohibited.

Her companion, realizing that no one seemed to pay any attention to the warning, shouted, "It's against the law to drink in public! Go home!"

Calixto, in an English mixed with a strong measure of Spanish, tried to explain to the officer that they were not bothering anyone, that they were simply gathered there to pass time. One of his companions, though, emboldened by the effects of the beer, pointed to the policewoman and said, in Spanish, "Go to Hell!"

The officers did not speak Spanish and therefore did not understand the drunken man's insult. But one of them insisted, "Stop drinking in the street, or we'll have to arrest you!"

Her insistence angered several of the men. Daniel tried to calm them down and started to approach the two women to explain the situation, but hearing his companions' loud and vulgar shouts, he changed his mind and returned to the group.

At that moment, according to the police report prepared by the Public Information Office, the agents "arrested two subjects for disorderly conduct and called for backup. Two uniformed officers from the Fourth District arrived to assist with the arrests."

Daniel complained to the police about the detention of his friends, and Calixto and the others did the same.

According to her statement to a local newspaper, Teresa, a mother of seven who at that moment was returning from her weekly grocery shopping, saw "two policewomen searching two Latino men, who were leaning against a phone booth with their hands up. Then a patrol car arrived and a tall policeman got out and began to beat one of the men with his nightstick."

"It was at that moment," stated the police report, "that a third subject showed signs of disorderly conduct, and a struggle ensued in an attempt to arrest him. While attempting to control the third subject, and before getting him handcuffed, the policeman was assaulted by a fourth subject."

"Then a great number of patrol cars arrived," stated Teresa. "And the police began to beat the people who had stepped in to defend the arrested man."

The policewomen then proceeded to arrest Daniel and, seeing this, Calixto and the other friends became angry and demanded that the police release him.

A beer bottle flew through the air and grazed a policeman's face. Daniel was trying to get away, but one policewoman had him with his hands behind his back while the other was preparing to handcuff him.

Meanwhile, attracted by the shouts and insults, several area residents came running to the scene of the disturbance and, together with Calixto and the other men who were gathered at the park, they surrounded the policewomen, who realized that the situation was becoming difficult and that it was necessary to act quickly and get out before tempers flared even more and the Latinos rioted.

Among the local residents who had congregated at the scene was a woman who knew Daniel. She began shouting loudly, demanding that the police release him. The policewomen were finally able to handcuff Daniel, but he was still putting up a struggle.

In the confusion one of the policewomen, a rookie, looked very nervous, giving the impression that she was about to explode in an attack of hysteria.

The commotion had grown and it appeared as though the neighborhood residents would not permit the police to arrest Daniel, who was still struggling and finally managed to free himself, momentarily, from the police.

"The man who was partially handcuffed," declared the report, "pulled a knife and threatened one of the policewomen several times."

"In the confusion the man ran toward the policewoman," declared Teresa. "I saw that both his hands were handcuffed, but I couldn't tell if he had a knife or not."

The rookie policewoman, seeing that Daniel was putting his hands into one of his pants pockets, believed he was pulling out a weapon and she immediately pulled her revolver and fired at close range.

"The officer pulled her gun while defending herself from the attacker," read the official report, "and she ordered him several times to drop the knife. When the man charged the agent, she was forced to open fire, shooting him in the chest."

"The officer told him to stop," declared Teresa, "and, when he didn't obey, she shot him, and he fell face down on the ground."

The loud gunshot frightened most of the people. The crowd dispersed. The other policewoman called for an ambulance. Meanwhile, unable to believe his eyes, Calixto observed the tragic scene a few steps away from his friend, who lay unconscious, bleeding heavily, sprawled on the hot pavement.

"During the incident," the official report documented, "one of the men who was originally arrested and handcuffed was able to escape."

Teresa stated that "although the man was bleeding, the ambulance took a long time to arrive."

20

"We're in Mexico City now," said the driver to one of the guides. "We've traveled about fifteen-hundred kilometers."

"Everything's gone pretty well so far," said the guide.

"The trip from the Guatemalan border to the capital took us twenty-four hours."

"Good work."

During the long journey, through most of which they tried to get some sleep, they had stopped for a short time at several places to eat and use the restrooms.

The bus stopped near the Central Camionera del Norte, one of the main bus terminals in Mexico City. One of the guides explained, "Okay, we're in Mexico City. This is another important point. This is where the going gets tough."

"Yes," said the other, "because the *migra* is really active from here to the U.S. border. That means this is where the exploitation and robbery begin. There's more risk of being caught."

"If you think that you've suffered on this trip so far, let me tell you, that was nothing! From here on out, our very lives are on the line."

"The bus station is three blocks from here. Right now it's exactly nine o'clock. We'll meet at the terminal at 11:30. The bus we're going to take will have a sign that says 'Ciudad Juárez.'"

"We can't be following every one of you around because we'll be noticed. So you have to be alert. The bus leaves at 11:30. So see what you can find to do for two and a half hours. Take a walk or get something to eat, but don't go far or you'll get lost. And don't drink. I don't want anyone showing up drunk. Don't talk much either, because your accent will give you away."

"When the time comes, make sure you know where the bus is. But don't get on until just a few minutes before it leaves. If you get on a half hour before, the *migra* will check and then you're screwed. When you see that the bus is ready to leave, that's when you get on."

"Okay, now, everyone out and we'll see you at 11:30."

The travelers abandoned the vehicle and walked toward the station in small groups. When Calixto, accompanied by Silvia, Elisa and José, entered the terminal, the first thing they noticed was several drunken beggars, barefoot and ragged, sprawled on the sidewalks. A strong stench had invaded the air they breathed. They heard a deafening hum, as if all the markets of the world were concentrated right there. Everything was being bought and sold. People moved back and forth tirelessly as in all bus stations, the only difference being that in this one the poverty appeared extreme and devastating.

For most of those travelers, simply arriving at that bus terminal made a tremendous emotional impact, although they had already gone through the extremely difficult experience of leaving their country. But now they had no alternative other than to bear the dismal panorama of the place and, at the same time, face the agony represented by the possibility of being discovered by the immigration authorities. They had to mix with the rest of the people and act normally to avoid calling attention to themselves.

Calixto's group had gone to have something to eat at a small café and through the windows they noticed some commotion in one area of the terminal.

"Maybe those guys are immigration agents," said Calixto, seeing some men hurry past, apparently chasing someone.

"Maybe they saw a group of *wetbacks*," said Silvia nervously.

Suddenly, whistles and shouts were heard. Several men and women ran, panic-stricken, past the café. The four travelers were tense, looking at each other, trying to hide the fear that their faces revealed.

"Poor souls," said José. "What bad luck."

"They may be Salvadoran too," said Elisa.

"Possibly," said Silvia. "They were dressed exactly like we are."

They left the restaurant and began to walk around the inside of the bus terminal.

"Let's just act like tourists," said José.

"Yes, let's walk calmly," advised Calixto, "but very alert to what's going on around us."

"Above all, we have to find the gate the bus leaves from," said Silvia.

"Yes," agreed Elisa. "That way we won't have to worry about that later."

"Fine," said José. "We'll do just that."

After walking around different areas of the station, Calixto found the bus and quietly said to the others, "Don't all look at once, but a little ahead of us, to the right, is the bus with the 'Ciudad Juárez' sign."

One by one they stole a glance toward the bus, and all agreed it was the one they were looking for.

"Good work, Calixto," said José. "It leaves in an hour."

"Let's keep walking around," advised Silvia. "I don't think we should stay right here."

Calixto noticed three of their travelling companions who were going back and forth from one place to another, apparently unable to locate the bus. He could see their desperation and knew that such an attitude could result in all of them being discovered.

They tried to approach Calixto to ask him, but he ignored them, suspecting that they were being watched. Calixto's group was calculating the time for boarding the bus. More members of their group walked by, obviously completely disoriented.

"What a difficult situation!" said José. "These poor people are lost and we can't help them because then we run the risk of getting caught."

"It's like a game of cat and mouse," said Calixto. "The *migra* is the cat and we're the mice. If we get the least bit careless, it catches us and eats us alive."

"But those people who are lost might ruin everything," said Elisa. "Maybe it's better to show them where the bus is."

"What if they catch all of us then?" asked Silvia. "Let's walk around again; maybe by the time we get back they will have found it."

Without any of the four noticing, six more of the travelers were following them around, forming a compact group of ten people. These people had placed a certain degree of trust in José since they had learned of the incident in the bar in Tecún Umán. One of them had been a soldier; now a deserter, during the trip he had developed a sense of camaraderie with José and Calixto, to whom he had related his escape from the army, thereby showing his trust in their friendship.

The soldier approached José. Silvia and Elisa already knew the man's story and, moved by the fear he inspired in them, withdrew a few steps and stood close to Calixto. José and the soldier continued walking at the front of the group.

The soldier looked desperate and said, "I've been looking for you everywhere! I was afraid your group was lost."

"No, we went to eat and then to find the bus."

"So you already know where it is?"

"Yes."

"Good, because if you didn't, I'd be glad to show you."

"Thanks."

"You're welcome," said the soldier with some satisfaction, and then added, "What a depressing place this is."

"Yes," agreed José, "as if the world ended here. And on top of that we have to be on guard so the *migra* doesn't catch us."

The soldier said nervously, "In my country I went through critical moments of life or death, but I was never in a situation as nerve-wracking as this one. I appreciate my life, but if they catch me here, I prefer to fight and let them kill me rather than be deported."

"Don't worry," said José. "Let's not panic; we'll just walk calmly, and they won't catch us."

"Thanks for your friendship," said the soldier. "I don't know why, but nobody on this damn trip inspires my confidence like you and Calixto."

The two men shook hands firmly to reaffirm their friendship and continued walking. Suddenly the soldier noticed several more of their traveling companions, who were desperately searching for the bus.

"Look at those poor people, abandoned, lost," he said. "They probably haven't found the bus."

"They'll find it soon," said José calmly. "Let's keep walking."

But the soldier was worried and suddenly decided that it was his duty to help those people, although doing so endangered his own chances.

"I've repressed people like that many times," he declared. "And I don't know why, but right now I feel I can't abandon them."

Then, moved by a paternalism toward those unfortunate souls, perhaps a product of his feeling of superiority over those who were in worse circumstances than he, the soldier announced, "If we'll all be screwed for helping those people, I don't give a damn. They're lost and we have to help them."

He walked toward the disoriented group. As he passed by, he asked for a cigarette, acting as though he didn't know them. Then, calmly, as he was lighting it, he said, "The bus is over there, on that side. Follow me."

21

JUDGE: Are you Teresa?

TERESA: Yes.

JUDGE: Do you speak and understand Spanish?

TERESA: Yes.

JUDGE: The person seated next to you is Ms. Smith. She is an attorney. Does she represent you in these proceedings?

TERESA: Yes.

JUDGE: Let the record show the presence of the respondent, her attorney, Ms. Smith, and the government's general attorney, Mr. Hammer. Very well, at this time, Ms. Smith, on behalf of the respondent, are you prepared to admit service of the Order to Show Cause, waive reading of the explanations required by regulation, admit the allegations of the Order to Show Cause, concede deportability and decline to designate a country of deportation–I will designate El Salvador–and apply for relief from deportation under sections 208(a), 243(h) and as an alternative 244(e) of the Act?

MS. SMITH: Yes, Your Honor, that is correct.

JUDGE: Thank you. I will mark the Order to Show Cause as Exhibit Number One and admit same into evidence. The file should note that the application for political asylum has been submitted and reviewed by the Department of State. The application has been admitted into the record as Exhibit Number Two. The State Department's letter is Exhibit Number Three. Ms. Smith, do you wish to interpose an objection to that letter?

MS. SMITH: Yes, Your Honor, I just received a copy of the asylum application last Friday and I noticed that it is incomplete, I suppose due to the circumstances under which it was prepared. For the record, I want to indicate that we will present new evidence and that we have already presented additional documents which support our case to rebut the opinion of the State Department.

JUDGE: Then, you object to admission of the letter into evidence?

Ms. SMITH: I object to the letter, Your Honor, only for the reason that it is a form letter which does not address the specific facts of the respondent's case.

JUDGE: Thank you. Exhibit Number Four has been submitted by the respondent. It is a combined exhibit which begins with material from the Americas Watch organization. Mr. Hammer, do you have any objection?

TRIAL ATTORNEY: No, Your Honor.

JUDGE: Exhibit Number Five is the government's exhibit which begins with an article on deported Salvadorans, reported by the newspaper Arizona Republic, together with two other things . . . Ms. Smith, do you object to the admission of these documents into evidence?

Ms. SMITH: No, Your Honor.

JUDGE: Thank you. For the record, Exhibit Number Three will be admitted into the record over objection. All remaining exhibits are admitted as well.

JUDGE: At this time, Ms. Smith, are you ready to proceed with your case?

Ms. SMITH: Yes, Your Honor.

JUDGE: Do you wish to call the respondent to testify first?

Ms. SMITH: Yes, Your Honor.

JUDGE: Teresa, please stand and raise your right hand. Do you swear or affirm that the testimony you are about to give in this proceeding will be the truth, the whole truth, and nothing but the truth, so help you God?

TERESA: Yes, sir.

JUDGE: Thank you. Come forward, please, and be seated. Ms. Smith, please proceed.

Ms. SMITH: Thank you, Your Honor. Teresa, would you please state where you are from, for the record?

TERESA: From El Salvador.

Ms. SMITH: What part?

TERESA: Cantón El Jocote, Municipio El Tránsito, San Miguel.

MS. SMITH: And when did you enter the United States?

TERESA: February 3rd.

MS. SMITH: On what date did you leave your country?

TERESA: Early in January.

MS. SMITH: Why did you leave?

TERESA: Because my life was in danger.

MS. SMITH: Why did you believe that you were in danger?

TERESA: Because we used to give water to the guerrillas.

MS. SMITH: Any other reason?

TERESA: Because the military . . . if the military found out we were giving water to the guerrillas, they would kill us.

MS. SMITH: How often did the guerrillas come to your house for water?

TERESA: Every week.

MS. SMITH: Why did they go to your house?

TERESA: Because our house was the first one.

MS. SMITH: First in what sense, near where?

TERESA: It was a road near a forest, near the path, so our house was near there.

MS. SMITH: Now, if this caused you to fear the military, why didn't you stop giving water to the guerrillas?

TERESA: We couldn't. If we denied them the water, they would kill us.

MS. SMITH: With whom did you live in your country?

TERESA: With my grandmother.

MS. SMITH: And your parents, are they both deceased?

TERESA: Yes.

MS. SMITH: Do you have a husband?

TERESA: Yes, although we aren't married.

MS. SMITH: How long have you been living with him.

TERESA: Eight or nine years.

MS. SMITH: Did you live with him in El Salvador too?

TERESA: Yes.

MS. SMITH: Did the guerrillas also come to ask for water at the house where you and your husband lived?

TERESA: Yes, because we had a barrel outside, and when they wanted water, they would ask us and then take it from there.

Ms. SMITH: Did that house belong to your husband?

TERESA: Yes.

Ms. SMITH: Did your husband come to the United States with you?

TERESA: Yes.

Ms. SMITH: Did he have any problems in El Salvador?

TERESA: Yes.

Ms. SMITH: What problems did he have?

JUDGE: Ms. Smith, how is this relevant? Are you going to demonstrate that she has the same problems as the husband due to the fact of living with him?

Ms. SMITH: Yes, Your Honor.

JUDGE: Fine, you may proceed.

Ms. SMITH: What problems did your husband have?

TERESA: He was in the military.

Ms. SMITH: Could you tell us the approximate dates of his military service?

TERESA: Around the end of 1981.

Ms. SMITH: Is that the time he entered the service?

TERESA: Yes.

Ms. SMITH: And when did he finish his military service?

TERESA: Early 1984.

Ms. SMITH: Why did he leave the military?

TERESA: Because the guerrillas threatened to kill him if he didn't leave the military. They had a list and photographs and they asked him if he knew the people who were on the list and in the photos. He said that all of them were in the military with him. Then they showed him a picture of himself. He wanted to deny it, but they said that if he did, they would kill him right there. They told him to abandon the military; otherwise he and his whole family would be killed.

Ms. SMITH: What was his response to them at that moment?

TERESA: First they told him they would give him a week to decide. He responded that he didn't need a week, that he was going to obey their orders immediately.

22

(Kitchen. Calixto, Caremacho, Juancho, Cali.)

Mother's Day is coming. I'm going to send Lina some money, so she can celebrate the day with our children.

I'm going to send some money to my mother too, so she can buy herself a little gift.

Me too. My mother will be so happy.

(*Calixto shows enthusiasm.*) My wife deserves a nice gift. She's a good wife.

You're lucky. You should take good care of her.

My little woman has been with me through all the difficult moments of my life, in good times and bad, without complaining, with patience and understanding.

How long have you been married?

Many years. I've lost count. I think fifteen.

In our countries women suffer more than men.

And here they work hard like men. My uncle lives with his family in Silver Spring. His wife cleans houses during the day, and when he comes home tired from his construction job, she makes him his lemonade and rubs his back. Then she prepares the meal. At the same time she's taking care of the two children so they won't make too much noise so my uncle can rest for half an hour. After supper, she goes off to work two hours at a part-time job cleaning office buildings.

There's no doubt that here women sometimes work harder than men, because they go to their job during the day and, when they get home, they have to take care of the children, the husband and the house.

In my hometown, the women work like beasts of burden, right alongside the men, harvesting cotton from dawn 'til dusk.

And on top of that, they pay them almost nothing.

The crew leaders and guards on the farms rape them, get them pregnant and don't take care of the children.

Many women are father and mother at the same time. Because often the men just get them pregnant and disappear.

Once with my own eyes I saw how a pregnant woman who was selling tamales, when she felt that she was going to give birth, put her basket on the ground, went off into the bushes and, with the help of another woman, had the baby right there. A little while later, she came out with the newborn crying in her arms; she picked up her basket, set it on her head and went on her way as if nothing had happened, calling out that she had salt and sugar tamales for sale.

The women in our countries are brave. They're very special people, aren't they?

Very special. That's why on Mother's Day I'm going to give a really nice present to my little woman.

What are you going to give her?

I'll send her some money so she can buy what she wants. And I'm going to send her a dress too.

That Calixto sure knows how to treat a woman!

I learned that in the country too.

23

The scene inside the bus station looked very dismal to the travelers. Night and day did not seem to exist. It was as if time had been suppressed there, or as if it were not measured by the hours shown on the clock but by the number of buses that entered and exited by the avenues that connected to the terminal like the tentacles of an immense octopus.

The travelers who stopped at that point every day in great numbers wore identical expressions of anguish, a result of the worry that at any moment they could be arrested, which would destroy their dreams of entering the nation to the north, the paradise they had imagined.

Two hours after Calixto and his companions entered the station, a group of travelers was detected by immigration agents. The alarming whistles accompanied by desperate screams were heard again. There was a commotion just a few yards away, and they saw how a large number of women, men and children ran haphazardly in all directions trying to escape, perhaps not even knowing where they were going, since all that mattered at that moment was evading the astute immigration agents. Some were arrested; others managed to escape and get out of the station.

That incident and the depressing panorama of the place increased the tension in Calixto's group. They moved to a different area of the station when they saw a policeman approach a man who was leaning against a post and ask to see his documents.

"You aren't Mexican," they heard the agent say. "You're under arrest."

"Poor man," said Calixto as he watched the officer escort the man whose face showed the resignation of defeat.

"If he pays a good bribe, they'll let him go," said the soldier.

"I wonder if they'll grab us when we get on the bus," said José. "Then we're done for."

"Maybe the *coyotes* already paid the required bribes," said the soldier. "They pay for the passengers to be left alone, and so the bus is allowed to leave without any problems."

"It's part of their business," said Silvia.

"Of course," said the soldier, "because it's impossible for them not to realize that certain buses are full of people who don't have papers even if we do get on just a second before it leaves."

"You can tell what we are a mile away," said Elisa. "We look like a handful of cornered animals."

"That's for sure. Look at those people that are lost, looking for the bus," said the soldier, pointing to a group that was going back and forth, desperately, through the terminal. "The fear and confusion are written all over their faces."

"I looked at myself in a mirror a few minutes ago," said Calixto. "And I saw the same look of panic on my own face."

"That's exactly why we have to try to act normally," advised Elisa. "Let's walk and talk as if we were just ordinary tourists."

They continued circulating through the station, conversing and forcing smiles, which looked more like fearful grimaces, since they had reached the conclusion that remaining in one place aroused more suspicion. Two or three times they passed by people they thought were immigration agents, who were posted near the ticket windows.

"When you buy your tickets," said Calixto, "remember what they told us, not to do it in groups, but first one or two people, then two more."

"José and Silvia go now," said Calixto. "Then Elisa and I."

The first pair headed for the ticket window, after walking by a couple of times in hopes of convincing any immigration agents that they were not trying to hide. Trying to look calm, they hoped to be taken for local residents.

The others did exactly the same thing. And when the whole group had acquired tickets, they kept walking.

"Let's not go far," said the soldier. "It's only fifteen minutes until the bus leaves."

"What luck that they didn't grab us," said José, "although I think the agents knew we didn't have papers and God only knows why they left us alone."

"Maybe they just decided not to arrest us," said Elisa.

"They indulged themselves" said the soldier. "They spared our lives."

"Yes, because it's obvious we're not an ordinary group," said Calixto.

"Of course, you can tell right away," said Silvia. "Just like that group over there in the corner. One look at them and you can tell they're headed to the North with the same intentions we have."

"Maybe the agents decide," said Calixto. "I bet they even enjoy it. They think: We'll arrest these and not those because farther on other agents will arrest them."

"That's right," said the soldier. "They've probably already communicated with the agents who are up ahead, telling them to wait for us and arrest us."

The music of countless jukeboxes formed a strange mixture of words and sounds. *Norteña* songs joined others with a southern style, and confusing messages of love, sadness, betrayal and disenchantment filled every corner of the Central Camionera del Norte.

"It's time to get on," said the soldier, "eleven thirty."

"Yes, let's go," said Silvia. "People are already boarding."

The group went toward the bus and got on. They took seats and, trying to hide their nervousness, anxiously awaited the moment it would finally abandon the terminal.

The driver's radio sang along with the voice of Javier Solís:

> Course not set, path unknown,
> where my ship will sail,
> I go only where destiny takes me
> and one day, yes one day, my ship will be
> the master of the sea . . .

In the business of the trafficking of undocumented persons, the Central Camionera del Norte represented the center of the world. All those headed to the United States stopped there, whether they were planning on crossing the border at Tijuana, Nogales, Ciudad Juárez, Piedras Negras, Nuevo Laredo or Matamoros; their final destinations included Los Angeles, Houston, Chicago, Washington and New York.

The walls and benches of the terminal witnessed so much sadness, despair and fear. They listened to the countless dramatic stories of the great Latin American exodus, the stories of millions of human beings who were fleeing from the misery and violence in their countries, in search of the promised land. Each traveler left a drop of suffering etched on the floor of that labyrinth as a living testimony of the painful odyssey toward the vast lands of the North.

When the bus finally abandoned the station, there was a general sigh of relief; the travelers closed their eyes, perhaps to secretly thank God and enjoy a private moment of celebration. As the vehicle pulled away they felt as if they were escaping from death itself.

At that moment Calixto remembered the words of the guide who, at the beginning of the trip, had said in an enigmatic voice, "If we get past the Central Camionera del Norte, we'll have almost made it." And Calixto thought to himself, "Yes, we've almost made it."

"Okay," said one of the leaders, "now the possibility of reaching the border is a little more reasonable."

"Yes," agreed the other, "because you can't even imagine the thousands of travelers who never even managed to reach the Central, and many thousands of others who never made it past the Guatemalan border. That's why we're lucky to have gotten this far."

They listened to the guide through yawns and the weariness that had overtaken them as a result of the many confused emotions they were experiencing.

The smuggler explained, "There are three main crossing points on the border. To the west Tijuana, in the center El Paso, and to the east Piedras Negras. We're taking the central route; our destination is Ciudad Juárez."

After a long trek, the bus entered a small, uninhabited town and stopped in front of a house that appeared to be deserted. They got out, their bodies numb, and took advantage of the stop to walk around a little and stretch their legs.

"We can't sleep here," said one guide. "We're just going to stop for an hour and a half to eat."

They entered the house, and an old woman and a young girl served them food, soft drinks and coffee.

"After you eat, go to the bathroom and take care of whatever you need to do," said the leader, pointing out the restrooms.

Exactly an hour and a half later, they got back on the bus and, once underway, one of the leaders said: "Okay, now we have to pass a rough place."

"Yes," said the other. "There are three security checkpoints that are heavily manned."

"And we have to pay a bribe at each one."

"We're spending a lot."

The rumble of the engine in the background interrupted the smugglers' words. Suddenly one of them stood up, holding on to the metal rails of the ceiling of the bus, as if he were a monkey in a cage, and said, "Now I'm going to explain to you what the deal is. We're going to need more money because we're spending more than the usual amount on this trip. So we need each of you to fork over another hundred dollars."

And with no further explanation, they began to collect the money from each of the passengers. They usually demanded three payments, in San Salvador, Guatemala and Mexico, and the rest before crossing the Rio Grande.

When they arrived at the first checkpoint, the bus stopped, a guide got out and returned after ten minutes. The same thing happened at the second one. But before reaching the third, the man said, "As you've seen, we've passed two police checkpoints and both times they let us through without any problem. And do you know why? Because I got out and paid a good bribe. But at the next one there's no such luck, because that's a real tough one. So to avoid the risk of having trouble, we're going to have to go around it."

"So when I give the word, you'll get out about a kilometer before the checkpoint, and go around it, through the desert."

"Don't let anyone see you. When cars go by, get down on the ground."

"Ten of you will stay on the bus so that it's not empty; that way it won't arouse the suspicions of the police."

The bus came to a halt and a leader chose those who had to get out. He divided them into small groups and pointed into the darkness: "There's the checkpoint. So you don't get lost, walk parallel to the highway, far from it, in the brush, until you pass the checkpoint."

"Yes," said the other guide, sticking his head out the bus window. "Go left as far as you can, but without losing sight of the highway or you'll get lost. This area is nothing but desert."

"And go in groups," continued the other. "Don't go all together. A group can start off every five minutes. And when you see a car coming, squat down or lie on the ground because, even though it's dark, the headlights can catch you and it'll be all over."

The man finished explaining, got on, and the bus pulled away. Those who had remained behind began their walk, eyes always on the highway, feeling their way over a bumpy path covered with thorny bushes.

24

DEATH TOLL 13 IN DESERT TREK OF SALVADORANS

AJO–The bodies of 10 more Salvadorans were found south of here yesterday, bringing to 13 the number of known dead from a group of at least 26 refugees abandoned by a smuggler in the scorching desert.

Thirteen refugees were hospitalized for severe dehydration or were in custody here, and 20 others were said to have planned to cross the border at San Luis, south of Yuma. Their fate is unknown.

Officials yesterday afternoon announced a halt to the two-day search that involved five helicopters, two light airplanes, four-wheel-drive vehicles, and motorcycles, combing the Organ Pipe Cactus National Monument area.

"There couldn't possibly be anyone out there left alive–we all know that," said Franklin Wallace, superintendent of the monument. E.J. Scott, senior patrol agent for the Border Patrol, said, "Anybody left out there was dead by noon (yesterday)."

Officials said the Salvadorans had entrusted almost $20,000 to a man who was to smuggle them to Los Angeles.

"The people that they paid to bring them through got their money and left," Wallace said. "They always do this. They left them stranded out there."

The dead and the survivors were found 10 to 20 miles north of the border. The dead found yesterday were discovered near a north-south power line running parallel and just a mile west of Arizona 85, the paved road from Ajo south to Lukeville.

Wallace said the temperatures Friday, Saturday and yesterday were 110, 106 and 103, "but that's in the shade, and who ever saw any shade around here?" The superintendent of the 516-square-mile monument said ground temperatures in the area reach 150 degrees.

"The eyes of the survivors were dead persons' eyes. The only thing they could say to us was '*agua*' . . . (they) were so close to passing away that it was just nip and tuck—we had lots of water

and we just poured it on them (to cool their body temperatures),"
Wallace said.

According to sheriff's officials, most of the travelers were
believed to have been from San Salvador, their country's capital.

The officials gave the following account of the journey to
Arizona:

Over a period of about five weeks, the Salvadorans had been
contacted by a man who offered to arrange transportation to the
United States. They were told that it would cost them $1,250 per
adult and $1,000 per child.

About 45 Salvadorans, almost all from middle-class back-
grounds, agreed to the deal and awaited further word from their
contact.

Somewhere en route, near the U.S. border, about 20 of the
passengers, mostly young children and women, disembarked from
the bus and found their way to San Luis, south of Yuma. It is not
known what has become of them.

After the remaining passengers were driven closer to the border, the driver herded them off the bus and said he would escort
them through the desert and across the border so that they would
not be detected by the Border Patrol, or other law-enforcement
agencies.

Somewhere along the way, the driver left his charges, telling
them he was going to get water and would return, but he never did.

The group, very few of whom knew each other, waited for
only a few hours and began the trek themselves. They had little
water or food, having been told that their fee included the price of
the life-saving substances.

Friday, authorities found several members of the group,
including a dead man.

Arizona Daily Star
July 7, 1980

25

News of the man shot by the police spread immediately, inflaming the tempers of the inhabitants and unleashing an unprecedented wave of disturbances in the neighborhood.

"Several people spread the false rumors that the wounded man was handcuffed with his hands behind his back and then shot," stated the police report. "This caused civil disorder in Mount Pleasant and surrounding areas."

Chaos invaded the streets, taking on violent dimensions, resulting in clashes between indignant demonstrators and police officers attempting to establish order.

That same night, a block from where the shot that wounded Daniel had been fired, the area of 16th Street and Lamont was crawling with policemen vainly attempting to retake control of the zone.

Helicopters flew over the neighborhood, trying to lend support to the squads of police who fired tear gas to disperse the large mob of demonstrators who, in response, threw rocks and bottles and then scattered in search of refuge.

The clashes were concentrated on Mount Pleasant Street. On one corner a huge bonfire burned, lighting up the whole neighborhood and completely consuming the Church's Fried Chicken restaurant. A block up the street, on the corner of Kenyon Street, the demonstrators discharged a torrential rain of projectiles on the 7-Eleven store and then looted it.

Several columns of anti-riot police attempted to stop the looting, arresting everyone in their path. This was the only way in which they were able to regain temporary control of the establishment.

Meanwhile, the occupants of the apartments situated along Mount Pleasant Street peered out of their windows, observing the spectacle of destruction enveloped in clouds of tear gas and smoke.

Moved by a strange party atmosphere, they played music: *salsa, merengue, rancheras* and *boleros*. Juan Luis Guerra, against a background of patrol car sirens and demonstrators' screams, sang:

> My *bilirubin* rises
> when I look at you and you don't look back
> and aspirin doesn't help,
> not even intravenous penicillin,
> it's a love that makes me spin
> my *bilirubin* rises . . .

The police brigades closed ranks and began to comb Mount Pleasant Street, from Irving to Park Road but, among shouts and whistles, the demonstrators bombarded them with whatever was handy and then dispersed, only to reappear behind the officers, frustrating them greatly. They had never imagined that in such a short time that tranquil place would become a war zone.

"It's like being in El Salvador," declared one resident. "This is like the battles we have all the time over there. Like when the government forces attack the political demonstrations to break them up, and the people respond throwing rocks and bottles to defend themselves."

At that moment, a light drizzle descended, as if spring also wished to make her presence known on that night unprecedented in the history of the neighborhood. A helicopter flew overhead, projecting a strong beam of light on the rioters. A hail of rocks and bottles fell on a column of police who had cleared the corner of Mount Pleasant and Kenyon. That set off another confrontation accompanied by explosions and clouds of tear gas. The demonstrators again scattered in all directions. A group of police officers returned to the 7-Eleven store, which by then had been completely looted.

The drizzle turned into a downpour, and perhaps the rain was the only thing capable of stopping the events of that tragic Sunday night, so violent and unexpected, which left a toll of several wounded, many arrests, and incalculable material losses.

26

The bus, now occupied only by the two guides, the driver and ten other persons, who paid an additional fee for not having to walk, resumed its trek on that intensely dark night crowned with a starry firmament. The walkers, meanwhile, without a guide or any light, spread out along an unfamiliar, rocky path, full of thorns and holes. Now Calixto understood why the guides insisted they wear long-sleeved shirts to protect their arms from the thorns. The path was not well-worn; they had to go through and over bushes and cacti. The women and children walked in silence along with the men.

Calixto was used to walking long distances, as it was the only form of transportation in his village, but he considered that walking in a stooped or crouching position was truly difficult. Although there was not much traffic on the highway that night, the walkers' fear of being discovered hindered their progress.

"Don't walk bent over," suggested José. "Walk upright and you'll see how much more comfortable it is. It's so dark no one will see us."

But no one paid any attention to him because their fear took over. José's group included Calixto, the soldier, Silvia, Elisa and a woman accompanied by an older man. They had walked for about an hour and a half and the thorns and their weariness were getting the best of them. They stumbled blindly, tripping with every step. Suddenly Elisa collapsed, groaned, and said "I can't stand it. I can't go on!"

Calixto helped her up. "Rest a minute; I'll stay with you."

"No, I don't think I can make it," she said. "I stepped in a hole and twisted my ankle."

"Here, lean on my shoulder," offered Silvia. "That way you can walk; we'll go slowly."

"No, I can't," insisted Elisa. "I'll stay here. You go on."

The soldier spoke up: "No way! No one is staying behind. Try to walk, just go slow. You can't really think we'd leave you here in the desert!"

Overcome by the intense pain, Elisa cried, "I can't walk anymore; I'll stay here."

The group that had begun the trek five minutes after they had caught up with them and continued on. The soldier approached Elisa and said categorically, "No, no one is staying behind."

"But I can't walk anymore," she said sadly.

"You'll forgive me for touching your legs," the soldier said resolutely, "but I'm going to carry you on my back."

He picked up Elisa, and they continued on their way. They passed the checkpoint and continued about a kilometer beyond, and stopped to wait for the bus.

Calixto remembered that in his village he walked a kilometer in fifteen minutes. But he calculated that, given the darkness and the condition of the path, it had taken them an hour to walk a kilometer.

After the three hours that journey on foot had taken them, their clothes were in shreds and their arms and legs were covered with scratches and bruises. The first group calculated that they had walked about a kilometer beyond the checkpoint and stopped as the guides had instructed. As the other groups arrived, they gathered in the darkness to wait, whispering to each other. Some were grumbling and others laughed nervously.

They had stopped near the highway, and when they did not find the bus that was to be there waiting for them, they began to wonder what could have happened.

"What should we do now?" someone asked.

A short, heavy man who, perhaps out of desperation and the uncertainty of the trip, had confided to the soldier his secret of having been an informer of a faction of the death squads, turned out to be the most fearful. He was saying, "Now they're going to capture us for sure!"

Several others ordered him to be quiet. About ten minutes had passed, which seemed like hours to the anguished travelers.

Silvia noticed that the night was so dark that the constellations could be seen clearly in the sky; the stars' shine was intense and they seemed very close to earth.

Suddenly, a light appeared in the distance. Immediately the walkers squatted down; some ran to hide but then returned, having realized that the area was flat and there was no vegetation. The light advanced toward them and suddenly stopped and went out. Everyone froze. The informer tried to flee, and said, "It must be the police; they've detected us and are coming to arrest us!"

"Silence!" begged a woman's voice.

One group took off running. Others wanted to follow but were paralyzed by their own indecision.

"Calm, please," said someone. "Don't scream and don't move. Don't be afraid; the bus will come soon."

The informer, fear-crazed, said, "It's the police. I'm going to turn myself in. They won't do anything to me because I have all my documents in order."

"It's the *migra!*" cried another.

And that statement made another group flee.

"Just sit down, please," begged a woman. "Calm down; everything will be all right."

But the informer insisted, "No, I have my documents here; I'm going to turn myself in."

One of the travelers noticed something that was coming from the place where they had seen the light go out. "It looks like someone's coming."

They fell silent. When the man drew near, they saw that it was one of the guides; the cast on his arm shone in the darkness. When he reached them, he asked, "How was the walk?"

No one answered. Seconds later someone said, "Some people ran away."

The man explained. "Those sons-a-bitches made us wait half an hour at the checkpoint. Then, on the road, a patrol stopped us, thinking we were drug smugglers. They kept us there about an hour and a half and didn't let us go until they had searched the bus inside and out."

Murmurs were heard a short distance away, and once the others realized it was the guide, they all talked out loud.

"Don't talk too loud," said the leader.

Some of those who had fled still had not appeared, and several men went to find them. They came back shortly with the stragglers.

The bus pulled up slowly and stopped in front of the group. Everyone got on. The guides made a quick inspection and counted the passengers to be sure that no one had gotten lost. The vehicle continued its journey, and a guide said, "I see you got a lot of thorns in your clothes, but don't scratch yourselves because that makes it worse; they get embedded in your skin. And then you're in for it, because they're so small that they stay in your skin for months no matter how much you scratch. It feels like thousands of tiny animals are eating you alive. I wouldn't wish it on my worst enemy."

"Don't worry," said his deputy. "At the next stop you can take a shower and clean off your clothes."

"Good. We made it. We've gotten past all the checkpoints. From here on out we'll rest; we'll be able to eat and shower."

"And we're heading for Ciudad Juárez," the other added somewhat enthusiastically. "Everything's gone like clockwork."

The passengers' good spirits returned. There were smiles and even jokes.

"You ran!" someone said.

"You fell!" said another.

"This guy was shitting in his pants, thinking it was the *migra*," joked one traveler.

"He definitely did," responded his companion, "because it stinks like shit!"

Loud laughter was heard immediately.

From that moment on the atmosphere felt less tense. The travelers regained the hope that soon they would reach their destinations. They were extremely tired but no one wanted to sleep because they wanted to share their experiences from the last stretch of the odyssey.

Elisa thanked the soldier for not abandoning her. "God will repay you," she said to him. "If you hadn't helped me, I might be lost who knows where!"

"Don't worry; it was nothing," he replied.

At the urging of several persons, the soldier was obligated to relate what had happened, which earned him the respect and admiration of all. A woman who was travelling with two boys asked him if he thought they were going to reach the other side of the border as they hoped. In an understanding and consoling voice, he said, "Don't worry, ma'am. You'll see; we'll be in the North very soon."

The woman seemed somewhat satisfied by the soldier's statement. Another declared, "Yes, we'll make it for sure, like he says!"

"Did you see how that guy ran?" someone asked mockingly.

They told jokes while attempting to extract the thorns from their skin and their clothing, but there were too many of them and they had to put up with them during the long journey whose distance was still unknown to them. Only the smugglers and the driver knew they were twelve hours from Ciudad Juárez.

It seemed to Calixto that this was the first time in the crossing that the travelers had smiled; this filled him with enthusiasm and renewed his hopes. They had passed the big test and overcome one of the greatest obstacles of the trip.

"From Ciudad Juárez to the border it's only a few kilometers," explained the leader. "So anyone who makes it to Ciudad Juárez is almost sure to get to the other side."

"But the *migra* is active there too, searching the hotels," said the other. "There's a chance of being arrested there; it's happened to many people. But even so, getting to that city is a victory, because there are thousands of travelers who have never made it that far."

"That's for sure. Getting north of Mexico City represents a great feat. And you've achieved it!"

Those words brightened the passengers' spirits even more; hearing them, they felt how close they were to the border.

"I've been caught twice," someone said. "And this is my last try, because I know very well that I'll never again be able to get the money for another trip. I've been arrested twice in Mexico, deported, and twice I've come back. The third time's the charm."

27

Ms. Smith: And did your husband actually leave the military?

Teresa: Yes.

Ms. Smith: Did he have any further encounters with the guerrillas?

Teresa: Yes. He was at a friend's wake, and when he was leaving for home, they stopped him near a fence. They told him to put his hands up and asked him what his decision was. They asked him if he was sure that he was going to leave the military and he said, yes, he was sure. "If not, you know," they said to him, "Your family will be in danger."

Ms. Smith: Did your husband return to the military after that?

Teresa: No.

Ms. Smith: Had your husband received any special training when he was in the service?

Teresa: Yes.

Ms. Smith: What was that?

Teresa: He received training here.

Judge: Excuse me, I didn't understand.

Ms. Smith: Her husband received military training here in the United States.

Judge: Fine.

Ms. Smith: What battalion did he belong to?

Teresa: I don't remember the name.

Ms. Smith: What was your husband's specialty? What work did he usually do in the army?

Teresa: He was part of a special battalion.

Judge: Had they been chosen to fight?

Teresa: Yes, to fight the guerrillas. He was a member of one of the battalions that were trained here.

Ms. Smith: What reputation did your husband have in the army?

TRIAL ATTORNEY: Your Honor, I don't understand how these questions are relevant . . . the questions about the husband's encounters with the guerrillas.

JUDGE: There's a thread; that's all I see. It's as if the guerrillas had said, "If you don't join us, we'll kill you and your whole family." Now, that's all we've gotten out of ten minutes of questioning. So, unless the husband's reputation can shed light on her situation in her country, I'd like to move on.

MS. SMITH: The reason I'm asking about this, Your Honor, is because I feel it corroborates why they had so much interest in him and why they insisted so much that he leave the military or they would kill him and his whole family.

TRIAL ATTORNEY: But he did leave . . .

JUDGE: Correct. The point is that he did leave, so we're going to go on from there. In other words, we have their message. Where is the evidence now? The husband received the message and left. He didn't need a week; he left . . . Very well, Ms. Smith, you may continue.

MS. SMITH: Teresa, did your husband tell the army that he was leaving?

TERESA: No.

MS. SMITH: Did they look for him when he did not return?

TERESA: Yes, they looked for him once or twice, but since we had moved from where we lived before . . .

MS. SMITH: To where did you move?

TERESA: To another town.

MS. SMITH: What's the name of the town?

TERESA: San Miguel.

MS. SMITH: Did you feel that you could continue living there without any problem?

TERESA: No.

MS. SMITH: Why not?

TERESA: Because there we were surrounded by the military.

MS. SMITH: And why was that dangerous for you?

TERESA: Because sooner or later, the guerrillas or the military would identify my husband, since both groups were looking for him.

Ms. Smith: What did your husband think would happen if the military found him?

Teresa: According to the law, he would be detained and imprisoned for five years, but he said that often they killed deserters.

Judge: Very well, just a moment. Ms. Smith, I don't know if we're hearing her case today, or her husband's, but we're far from the central point. I would like to know why she is afraid of being persecuted in El Salvador, and I have not yet found the reason. After fifteen minutes of questioning there is nothing more than the fact that the guerrillas once threatened that if he didn't leave the army, he would be killed. He knew that he would go to prison and all the rest but . . . this hearing is not about his case but about hers.

Ms. Smith: Yes, Your Honor, that is true. May I make an offer of proof?

Judge: Please.

Ms. Smith: The two main bases of her case are the assistance provided to the guerrillas and essentially her husband's case. And to the extent that it affects her, we would like to be able to present evidence on it. Her husband's concern with regard to the military, since apparently he was very much respected and very skilled when he was in the army, is that they were going to continue to be interested in him and that, if they found him again, his fear is that the guerrillas would believe he had surrendered voluntarily to the military and then the guerrillas would take reprisals against Teresa.

Judge: Did anything like that happen?

Ms. Smith: No, the husband left . . .

Judge: I mean, to her . . .

Ms. Smith: No.

Judge: Then we are dealing with her fear and her speculations about an event which may or may not have happened. From what I understand, that event did not occur.

Ms. Smith: Correct. We're dealing with her fear of returning to her country.

Judge: It's her fear. Subjective fear. You know her subjective fear is irrelevant unless you can show that she has objective facts to substantiate the subjective fear . . .

Ms. Smith: Correct. It's true that up to this point it is his case and the objective facts are the threat that they would kill his family, and in that way it affects Teresa.

Judge: Fine, I will allow you to offer evidence on the fact that the military or the guerrillas were going to kill his family, or not even kill his family, that they were going to harm her as a member of that family. If you can show that, fine; but if not, I'm going to have to prohibit that entire line of questioning.

28

(A crowded restaurant. Calixto, Juancho and Caremacho are discussing, among other things, Independence Day.)

Speaking of Independence Day, the reason for the celebration has never been very clear to me.

I remember September fifteenth because on that day they used to give out candy at school after we sang the National Anthem.

I remember one time in school they made us march in a parade. The soldiers from the barracks prepared us; they taught us the goose step.

What's that?

A way of marching where you step with your legs stretched out. They told me not to come to school barefoot that day because it was a disgrace to the country to march barefoot on that sacred day.

So you didn't march, Calixto?

They also told us that no one could be absent and my dad had to borrow money to buy me a pair of huge shoes that looked like tanks, and socks that came up to my knees.

You must have looked really elegant in your new shoes!

It was the first time in my life that I wore shoes.

Where was the parade? At the school?

No, it was on Main Street, a dusty street full of holes. We marched in the scorching hot sun at noon.

Did you sweat a lot?

I fainted.

Probably the hot sun made you sick.

I don't know what made me sick. But I remember that all of a sudden my stomach started to hurt a lot, maybe because the beans didn't sit well that morning. My shoes gave me blisters because they were way too big for me. My socks ripped.

That was your first parade.

First and last. Because the following year they didn't have one.

Why not?

Because too many students had fainted the year before. So the school principal said we were lazy and that we didn't deserve to march on Independence Day.

Why did so many faint?

One of the teachers said that we fainted because we were undernourished, and that instead of making us march in the hot sun, that the school should help us to get better nutrition and at least give us a glass of milk every day. The principal didn't agree with the teacher and fired him, and nobody else said anything. And that's what comes to my mind when I hear people talking about Independence Day.

I remember that in school they taught us the major events that happened during independence. And they taught us the words on the National Coat of Arms: "God, Union and Liberty." But the truth is I don't understand the meaning.

(*A waitress approaches. Caremacho looks at her curiously.*)

Bring us more *pupusas* and beer, please.

Okay. I'll be back in a few minutes.

(*The waitress leaves their table. Caremacho hasn't taken his eyes off her.*)

She's pretty . . . Well, I don't understand much about national holidays either.

In the capital there's Independence Avenue. And there are lots of prostitutes there.

But I don't think Independence Day is to celebrate those women.

No, man. September fifteenth is the day our country became independent from Germany.

No, man. You guys don't know anything about history. It was September 15, 1821, that we became independent from Spain. I bet you don't know who the founding fathers are either.

I remember that in school they told us about Matías Delgado, a fat little priest with a big nose.

José Simeón Cañas freed the slaves, didn't he?

That's right. And Santiago José Celis, another of the founding fathers, died in a jail in Ahuachapán.

Why?

I don't remember. But another founding father named Pedro Pablo Castillo, who didn't agree with the others, was exiled and died in Jamaica.

Independence Day brings a bunch of mixed-up ideas to my memory. I'd like to know the true reason for the celebration.

(*Caremacho observes a man.*) Look at that guy. He's had too much to drink.

(*All eyes turn to an individual who, staggering, approaches the jukebox, which contains typical Salvadoran songs: "El Carbonero," "Acajutla," "Un rancho y un lucero," and others, even the National Anthem. The man chooses the National Anthem and as soon as he hears the introduction he begins to cry, struggling to keep from falling, and assumes a position of military salute. Moved by his attitude and the familiar strains, others stand and, off-key but with great respect and enthusiasm, amid noisy hiccups and sneezes, they chorus the few words they remember.*)

> Let us salute our Fatherland
> proud to call ourselves its sons,
> and spiritedly swear the ceaseless consecration
> of our lives to its good.

29

They checked into an old hotel located on the outskirts of Ciudad Juárez. The leader said, "You stay here. Don't go out because they're always searching the streets in this area. When we come back we'll bring food."

"We'll be back soon," said his assistant. "We have to go arrange for the border crossing."

Two days passed and the men still had not returned to the hotel, two long days in which the travelers remained locked in the dark rooms of that run-down hotel, with nothing to eat. On the third day, overcome by hunger, the soldier left his room and knocked on the door of the room where Silvia, Elisa, Calixto and José were staying. Calixto opened the door a crack and the soldier said to him, "This is ridiculous! We're starving and those bastards haven't shown up. Let's go buy some food."

"Okay, let's go," said Calixto. "No problem."

They agreed that they would first walk around the neighborhood to familiarize themselves with the place and then buy only as much as necessary, to avoid arousing suspicion by carrying a lot.

They entered a modern, well-stocked supermarket, where they made their purchases. They made it back to the hotel with no problem and distributed the food to the members of the group. The food did not completely satisfy their hunger, but it was enough to allow them to recover their vital energy.

Everyone thanked the soldier and Calixto for having risked being arrested or getting lost in a strange town to bring them the food.

The next day, four days after they had left the group, the guides appeared. Seeing that the travelers had eaten, they could not hide their surprise. One of them asked, "Who fed you?"

At that moment the soldier, furious, answered, "Well, you son of a bitch, do you think I was going to starve waiting for you? Quit screwing around, it's your job! You said you were going to bring food and you didn't show up for three days. What kind of shit is that? You bastards don't care if people starve to death!"

The complaint was echoed by other travelers who, influenced by the soldier's anger, began to express their own grievances.

"Okay, okay, don't get so upset," said one of the guides. "We had serious problems, but we're here now."

"Don't worry," said the other. "I'll be right back with some food."

One of them left the hotel and returned half an hour later with plenty of food, which he distributed to the still-hungry travelers. When they finished eating and it seemed that their tempers had calmed down, one of the guides went room to room saying, "Tonight we're crossing. Get ready."

Night fell and all the members of the group were prepared to leave, but one of the guides announced, "We have problems. We can't cross tonight."

"We have to wait a few more days," said the assistant. "We were just informed that the Border Patrol is very active right now. It's best to wait and not take chances."

"And don't anyone dare go out on the street, because they've stepped up the search for undocumented people."

Tension gripped the travelers again because of their prolonged confinement, hunger, desperation and the terrible stories that some of them were telling. One man, who said his name was Armando and that he was from Santa Ana, commented, "I've tried to cross the border several times and I've had the bad luck that they've always caught me and deported me."

Another traveler said, "I got caught too and spent eight months locked up in a Mexican jail because I couldn't get the money I needed for them to let me out."

They spent several more days confined in the hotel. Every day the smugglers gave them a different explanation for the delay: "The contacts on the other side aren't ready yet." The next day they would say, "This isn't a good night because the place where we're going to cross is being watched." And the following day: "Some of your relatives haven't deposited the money with our contacts in the United States yet."

The soldier did not trust them and, on the sixth day of the wait, commented to the others, "These bastards aren't taking us across because every night they go out and have a great time at the bars and brothels, enjoying the night life."

A week after they first arrived in Ciudad Juárez, one of the guides finally declared, "We've just been informed that the friends and relatives of all of you have finally paid our contacts the other half of the cost of the trip."

"Everything's ready," said the other. "Tonight, for sure, we cross."

An unusual atmosphere of enthusiasm invaded the group and many of the travelers, unable to contain their emotions, nervously paced the hotel's narrow hallways.

The members of the soldier's group, nevertheless, lay resting on the small beds that barely fit in the tiny, dark room. One of them was the informer, a nervous, distrustful man who was always attentive to the least bit of noise in the hotel, to the point that at night it was impossible for him to fall asleep, as if his remorse would not let him rest. Huge dark circles surrounded his eyes. The other member of the group was a silent, hermetic man, who had not said one word during the entire journey, as if he were the bearer of a state secret and feared revealing it if he opened his mouth. The third was a young man from Santa Ana, whom they called simply Santaneco. Unlike the rest, he talked excessively; it seemed to the soldier that he would never be quiet.

"They say there are a lot of casinos here in Ciudad Juárez," said Santaneco.

"I don't know," said the soldier. "I don't know anything about this city. It's my first time here."

"On the last trip, while we were waiting to cross the border, like we are now, one of the travelers decided to go out and walk around."

"That's very dangerous," commented the informer.

"That's what we told him," clarified Santaneco. "But the man went out anyway, to the casinos, to bet the little bit of money that he had."

"He must have lost everything," said the soldier.

"On the contrary! He came back to the hotel so happy because he had won a small fortune! And right there he decided to return to his country and start a business, since he had already gotten what he hoped to find in the North, without even having to cross the border!"

"What luck," commented the informer.

Santaneco went on: "I, on the other hand, continued on only to be caught and arrested. Like they say, 'Some are born under a lucky star, others cursed.' When they deported me I went to visit the man who had won the money. He had prospered. And since we had become good friends and I reminded him of his good luck, he lent me the money for this trip."

"When I was in the military," said the soldier, "I heard about a man who came back before crossing the border too."

"Did he win money at the casinos?" asked the informer.

"He didn't go to the casinos but to the brothels," said the soldier. "And what he got was an infection. He got so sick so fast that he couldn't continue on the trip and was forced to go back home. And over there they took him right to the hospital. Months later they discovered that he was infected with the AIDS virus."

"Here at the border you can find your fortune but also your death," declared the informer.

At that moment Santaneco got up and left the room, saying he was going to the restroom. The informer said he would go with him. The soldier and the mysterious man were left alone.

"What about you, do you have family on the other side?" the soldier asked somewhat indifferently, assuming he would receive no response.

But, perhaps burdened by the loneliness that made everyone talk sooner or later, the fellow said, "I don't have anyone."

"Then, where are you going?"

"I'm not planning to stay there and work like the rest of you."

"I can't believe you'd subject yourself to this hard trip unless it's to make a better life for yourself."

"I'm going to do something else."

"What's that?"

The man hesitated for an instant, then responded, "To avenge the death of a relative."

"What?!"

"To find the man who killed my brother."

"Son-of-a-bitch!" exclaimed the soldier. "Those are serious words!"

"That's right. Some go north in search of life. But I'm going in search of death. And anyone who gets in my way I'm taking with me."

"Wow, my friend. I wouldn't want to be in the shoes of the guy you're looking for, not even in my dreams!" The soldier could not believe the man's words, but did not want to argue with him. "Look, friend, it's your life, and only you are responsible for it and for your actions. As far as I'm concerned, the only thing I want is to cross the damn border and begin a new life. The rest doesn't interest me."

The man, showing no emotion, commented enigmatically, "Like the song says, 'To each his own life, to each his own cross.'"

30

SURVIVORS TORTURED
BY THIRST

The survivors of the group of undocumented persons abandoned in the Arizona desert south of Ajo were forced by thirst to drink their own urine, shaving lotion and deodorant, and suffered wounds from every species of cactus known to the desert.

"Feeling tormented by the extreme desert heat, they had taken off their clothing," stated the doctor of the New Cornelia Hospital, where authorities had transported them. "They had thorns stuck in their feet, backs, legs, and faces–everywhere you can imagine."

There was time for only a cursory examination of the survivors, because their immediate problem was dehydration. "Some of them figured out how to drink the moisture from cacti; they were the smart ones," said the doctor, who prescribed intravenous glucose and all kinds of rehydration fluids.

Five survivors were discharged from the hospital early yesterday, but three women were still in intensive care. "They are all in serious condition, but I'm sure they will survive," predicted the doctor.

"Something must be done to keep these poor people from trying to cross the desert in the summer heat without water. These people were not riffraff, but appeared to be people of some means, of the middle class," said the doctor. "They had Mexican and U. S. money with them."

One of the women confessed that she could not return to her native land "because her life was in danger." She also stated that they had been wandering in the desert for "three to four days."

The Arizona Eye
July 8, 1980

31

On Monday night, Mount Pleasant Street again became the center of attention, and violence, in Washington, and consequently in the international news, perhaps because it was an unexpected event which took the very capital of the United States by surprise. Images of the looting and burning of the Church's Fried Chicken restaurant the night before remained vivid in the minds of the surprised neighborhood. The rioters had destroyed the building completely, stealing all the chicken, cooked and frozen.

In the early evening hours some of the community leaders tried to defuse the situation and offered to intercede between police and demonstrators, but it was obvious that nothing and no one was capable of containing the wave of disturbances that lay in store for the Adams Morgan area that night.

Already visible were the remains of a bus abandoned by its terrified passengers and driver when a mob had stopped it and discharged their anger by breaking the vehicle's windows.

The confrontation began when several bottles were thrown at the line of police, who responded with tear gas. The demonstrators fled.

At that moment violence broke out again in the neighborhood, which was suddenly invaded by gangs of young Latino men followed by black Americans, unleashing a wave of vandalism and looting in the majority of the businesses on Mount Pleasant Street and Columbia Road.

The terror reached its climax and the place showed an incredible panorama of destruction. The blind, violent crowd continued to loot and burn every establishment it came across. The Embassy Drugs Pharmacy suffered numerous assaults. The rioters put up barricades in the street and then set fire to them. Columns of police appeared, throwing tear gas grenades to disperse the crowds, but every time they left to deal with problems in other sectors of the city, the gangs returned.

A patrol car attempted to break through one of the barricades, but an explosion followed by an enormous fire stopped it. A policeman jumped out of the car, pistol in hand, and at that moment a bottle struck him in the head with such force that he fell to the ground and was barely able to call for help using his radio.

One of the gangs broke the windows of a laundromat and then burned it down. Enormous multicolored flames engulfed the place; they were finally extinguished by water from five firetrucks.

At midnight the neighborhood again revealed the dismal and desolate image of a battlefield: streets full of burned vehicles, destroyed businesses, flaming barricades and the strong stench of tear gas.

Little by little the authorities began to retake control of the area, not by force nor through their skill but rather because the rioters apparently had satisfied their thirst for violence that night and had left the neighborhood.

A curfew took effect. That night the disturbances had extended to other areas, which by then also had looted and destroyed businesses.

32

At eight o'clock at night the guides gathered the group, and one of them said, "Okay, it's time to get rid of everything. You'll cross with just the clothes you're wearing. Everything else, including your luggage, stays here."

Silently they went out into the dark, deserted street. Here and there a dog barked in the distance. Four taxis, headlights out, pulled up and the travelers got in quickly.

"Get down!" ordered the smugglers. "Don't let your heads show!"

They put seven people in each vehicle; those that did not fit were put into the trunks. One of the guides walked around the cars, examining them from a short distance, to make sure that the passengers could not be seen; then he got into the lead car and gave the order to proceed.

After travelling for about twenty-five minutes through the outskirts of the city, they pulled up next to a dark field and everyone got out. Three of the taxis disappeared and one remained behind, as if it were waiting for someone. Three men appeared out of the brush. The guide divided the travelers into three groups and assigned each of them to one of the men.

"From now on each group will be led by one of these guides. Do what they tell you and everything will go fine." The guides wore backpacks and dark caps.

The smuggler then took aside two young women who were traveling alone and said, "You'll cross with us."

The women joined them, somewhat surprised, but resigned to their fate.

The smugglers got in the taxi with the two women and the car pulled away. One of the remaining guides explained quietly, "Okay, this is where we start running, and anyone who doesn't keep up will get left behind. Don't talk; don't say a word. If someone falls behind and you want to help them, you're risking your life and the life of everyone in the group, because we won't wait for anyone. Now follow us."

And without further explanation, the men took off running like rabbits entering the field in three different directions. The groups ran after them, trying to keep them in sight. They could hear dogs barking. At times the guides stopped and crouched down, and everyone else did the same. They appeared to be awaiting some kind of signal, and then they continued running. This went on for about fifteen minutes; during that time helicopters flew over them twice.

The area was thick with prickly pear cacti and other thorny plants. Helicopters flew over, shining strong spotlights toward the ground. A small plane passed over also; lying on the ground among the bushes, they waited for the planes to leave the area. The guide finally gave the signal and they continued on.

Finally they reached the Río Bravo, known as the Río Grande on the other side, and crossed at a shallow place, where the water came up to a little above their waists.

When they arrived on the other side they saw a small hill right in front of them. The first to climb it were the three guides. They disappeared for a moment, as if they were looking for something. They returned a few seconds later, running down to the groups who were waiting nervously. One of the guides ordered, "Let's go, everybody, hurry up!"

They obeyed the command and scrambled up the hill. The first thing they noticed on the other side was a paved highway, illuminated by weak, yellow lights. Finally they were in the United States!

Someone complained of having lost a shoe. One woman shivered from the cold; she had slipped on a stone while crossing the river and was completely soaked.

"Don't worry; you'll dry," said one of the guides. "Now you see why they call people who cross the border illegally 'wetbacks.'"

Hidden behind thick brush on the other side of the highway, awaiting the travelers, were two vans. The guides ordered the group to get in immediately. Some sat down on the floor of the vehicles as others fell on top of them, leaving everyone in awkward, uncomfortable positions.

"Don't let your heads show through the windows," said one of the men.

Two of the men who had crossed with the group got into the vans with the driver. The third went back the way they had come.

At that moment the guide and driver of the vehicle in which Calixto, Elisa, Silvia, José, the soldier and the rest of their group of fifteen were travelling, decided what route they would take. The driver said, "We'll take the desert side, to Silver City. The other van will go a different way."

The vehicle pulled away, maintaining a moderate rate of speed so as not to arouse suspicion. They had travelled for about two hours when a women yelled that she had to go to the bathroom and asked them to stop. One man began to vomit. Another said he could no longer stand the uncomfortable position in which he was riding.

Calixto was sitting on the floor of the van, leaning sideways so his head could not be seen through the windows. Several people were lying on top of him and he was having trouble standing their weight; his legs had fallen asleep.

The guide and driver, strangers to the group, appeared extremely nervous. The ones who had accompanied the travelers to Ciudad Juárez had remained behind with the two women who supposedly were going to cross the border with them.

The guide's only concern was that the travelers' heads not show through the windows. But some of them could no longer stand their uncomfortable positions. Several had vomited on their companions. After three hours the guide said, "We're going to stop once, just for a minute, so you can get more comfortable and anyone who needs to can go to the bathroom."

They stopped in a dark, deserted area. After a minute everyone got back in, piling on top of each other as comfortably as possible. The guide asked them to be completely quiet, and they continued on.

A short time later one of the travelers became very nervous and, in his desperation, wanted to smoke. They told him not to, but he lit a cigarette anyway. The guide ordered the driver to stop, made the man get out and said, "If you don't put that shit out and sit still, I'll leave you here in the desert!"

Finally the man obeyed and got back into the van, clenching an unlit cigarette in his teeth.

They continued their journey and after another hour arrived in Silver City, New Mexico, where they stopped at a gas station.

33

Compañera Tzu-Nihá:

I'm writing this quick letter with great emotion, as we take a short break from a difficult guerrilla operation. Our mission was to attack and keep under fire an army battalion that watches the mountain where our base is located; meanwhile a group of our *compañeros* was escorting a wounded commander. After a long walk, amidst bombs and bullets, the group escorting the commander descended the mountain and continued on its way toward the city where the commander will receive assistance. We suffered two casualties and several wounded; they had many more.

But, beloved Tzu-Nihá, in spite of how difficult the war is, everything takes on a feeling of hope when I think about our love, about the day we met, about the missions in which we fought side by side, about the sacred moment when we chose our names Tzu-Nihá and Tzi-Vihán in memory of our Mayan ancestors, and swore our love to each other forever, and that together we would fight for social justice. And that, in spite of your absence, *compañera*, is what inspires me to fight with courage and dignity, to continue on in pursuit of the vindication of our glorious people.

I observe the mountain's splendor and wonder how you are and in what distant land you may be. And I want to tell you, *compañera* of my soul, that the images of your departure are still vivid in my mind, the instant when we said "until forever," the last warmth of your hands caressing mine, the certainty in your eyes when you told me, "I love you," your sad smile when you told me, "Goodbye." But I find consolation in believing that all this is just a small detour in the infinite path of our love . . .

Well, beloved Tzu-Nihá, the break has ended, the people call, the war continues. Nevertheless, the inextinguishable flame of our love also continues. Write me at the agreed-upon address.

"The people will overcome."

Tzi-Vihán

34

(*Kitchen. Calixto, Cali, Caremacho, Juancho, Chele Chile.*)

The first days I was here in the United States, I didn't even go out of the apartment.

Why is that, Calixto?

Because I was afraid of getting lost or getting caught. It took about a week for me to get up the courage to go out and walk around the building.

What did you do when you met people? Did you say hello?

No way! When I saw someone coming I'd cross the street for fear that they were Immigration agents who would arrest me on the spot.

Their agents aren't all white men. There are blacks and even Latinos.

That's right. That's why, when I first got here, I didn't trust anyone.

But you had to go somewhere sometime. You couldn't spend your whole life cooped up in your apartment.

The first time I went out was when I couldn't stand the cramped quarters and bad smell in the apartment, and so I went to spend the night in the basement of a building they called El Barco.

The one that was on the corner of Calvert and Adams Mill?

That's the one. I spent the night there but I didn't dare even close my eyes for fear that I'd be attacked.

Drunks and homeless people slept there.

And to make matters worse, it got really cold that night, and by morning I had a cold.

Things went from bad to worse.

And when did you find your first job?

That was the hardest part. I spent two months looking, until finally I found a job washing windows on buildings, something I had never done.

Weren't you afraid of being up so high?

At first I was. But needing the job made me brave. We didn't have the right equipment; we just tied ropes around our waists to go down from the roof of the building to the windows, sticking to the walls, hanging on anywhere we could.

You must have looked like an iguana, Calixto.

That's right. An iguana with its tail hanging out in the air. But that little job didn't last long.

Why's that? With so many buildings with hundreds of windows here in Washington, there's more than enough of that kind of work!

Well, what happened is that once in a while we were washing windows, my co-worker's rope broke, he fell straight down and ended up like a tortilla on the sidewalk. The police came and I had to take off because I was afraid they'd blame me.

How awful!

That's nothing. Back at the apartment, when the manager of the building found out that there were twenty tenants living where supposedly there were only three, he evicted the guy who had rented the place and gave him a week to leave.

So did you go live at El Barco?

I almost did. I had no alternative. I was out in the street. I got so desperate I decided I should go back to my country, but I didn't have enough money to buy the ticket.

Bad luck.

That's for sure. But fortunately the next day I found this job here; and before the week was out one of my cousins who has his whole family here, the same one who helped me post bond so the *migra* let me out, took pity on me and gave me a place to stay.

That was a stroke of luck.

You'd better believe it!

35

SOLDIER X:
UNDOCUMENTED FUGITIVE

An undocumented Salvadoran army deserter, who identified himself as a former member of the death squads, in which he operated under the pseudonym of Soldier X, has requested political asylum in the United States.

In an exclusive interview, Soldier X stated that he served two years in the army, where he belonged to a special battalion that received military training in the United States. He claimed to have joined the death squads voluntarily and served four months in a paramilitary group.

In the interview, Soldier X described a murder in which he participated as a death squad member:

> Somebody brought us an order containing the description of an individual accused of hiding guerrillas in his home. Dressed in civilian clothes and masks, we got into a van with tinted windows and no license plates and went to the home of the accused.
>
> When we entered the house, he started to run, but desisted when he saw several Uzis aiming at him. We arrested him and took off. In the van, we tortured the man in several different ways, including using the *capucha,* a hood filled with quicklime. We pulled it over his face, temporarily asphyxiating him, and then removed it to continue our interrogation. But the suspect refused to reveal anything at all. We took him to a remote place on the outskirts of the city and shot him, as we had done with so many others.

Soldier X also declared that his unit participated as reinforcements in the El Calabozo massacre:

> According to our information, there was a guerrilla training camp there. But when we arrived in the area, it was all over. We saw many dead bodies of women and children. Many others were near death.

Soldier X stated that once when he was attending a wake in his home town, the guerrillas stopped him, threatening him that if he did not leave the army they would kill him and his family. He promised that he would desert immediately. A short time later he assumed a false identity and, along with his wife, joined a group of undocumented travelers headed by smugglers who would transport them to the United States. The group was captured at the border and jailed; later some of its members, including Soldier X, were released on bond. After living and working for a time in Maryland, Soldier X traveled to El Paso to post bond for his wife, but she had already been deported to her country, where she was mysteriously murdered.

"I've had a long time to think about what is happening in my country, about all the things I did, and about my wife's murder. I don't want to be on the run anymore."

Regarding his application for political asylum, Soldier X declared: "If I returned to my country I would meet the same fate as my wife, since the guerrillas as well as my former colleagues in the death squads would certainly try to eliminate me."

The Los Angeles Watch
November 18, 1986

36

Five hours from the border, two hours after going through Silver City, the travelers were intercepted by a patrol car, which turned on its siren and flashing lights. A voice over a megaphone ordered them to stop. The driver ignored the order and turned the van off the highway and into the desert at top speed, with the patrol car, its sirens screaming, in hot pursuit.

The driver stopped the vehicle abruptly, jumped out and fled on foot into the desert, throwing the keys into the bushes. The guide fled in the opposite direction.

The officer who had stayed with the travelers while the other pursued the driver shouted an order in Spanish: "I'm an Immigration officer. Wait in the vehicle and don't move!"

Those words crushed the spirits of the travelers. Some began to cry; others cursed the moment in which they decided to embark on the trip, since in spite of having gotten the money to pay for it with so much sacrifice and in spite of all the suffering along the way, everything had ended without their having achieved what they so strongly desired.

The driver was finally captured. The guide managed to escape. By then, other patrol cars had arrived on the scene, which was suddenly illuminated by the powerful lights of a helicopter whose engine added noise and confusion to the dramatic scene of the capture.

Several agents rushed back and forth, making sure the travelers were properly handcuffed, and then ordered them into other vans in groups of seven.

They were captured around one o'clock in the morning and taken to a station at which they were transferred to large buses with bars on the windows. They then embarked on a long journey, stopping once at what appeared to be an intermediate point, where they were given sandwiches and soft drinks. From there they began the journey to El Paso.

Along the way they picked up other prisoners who had been captured at different points along the border; in all there were a total of five buses full of undocumented persons proceeding in caravan to El Corralón, the largest Immigration and Naturalization Service detention center on the border. They reached their destination at about five o'clock in the afternoon, nineteen hours after their initial detention.

In El Corralón the travelers were photographed and information taken for files which were opened on each of them. At that time they were given the opportunity to make a telephone call to a relative or friend. They were forced to sign documents, many of which they did not understand. Then they were transferred to the main prison.

Men, women and children from all over the world were detained at El Corralón. Calixto's group was taken directly to a soccer field on the prison grounds. From there they could see the nearby El Paso airport and watch the planes take off and disappear into the sky; the detainees hoped they would one day fly in those planes, going far away from that prison.

The detention center received its Spanish nickname of "Big Corral" from Mexicans who were held there in large numbers for crossing the border illegally.

37

Ms. Smith: Thank you, Your Honor . . . Teresa, why did your husband take seriously the guerrillas' threat that they would kill his family if he continued in the military service?

Teresa: Because that's what they would do.

Ms. Smith: How do you know that they would do it?

Teresa: Because whatever they promised they would do, they always did.

Ms. Smith: So you know of cases in which such threats were carried out?

Teresa: Yes, because those who had been warned to leave the military and didn't do so, the guerrillas killed them.

Ms. Smith: And why did the two of you believe that you could not continue to live in your country without the military finding and detaining your husband?

Teresa: No, we couldn't live there because he was in danger from both sides.

Ms. Smith: Did you move to a different area?

Teresa: Yes.

Ms. Smith: To where?

Teresa: To the capital.

Ms. Smith: Did you feel safe living there?

Teresa: No, because I didn't know anyone. And my husband felt that everyone there was suspicious of him, even though he was familiar with the area.

Ms. Smith: Did he used to live there?

Teresa: At one time he was stationed there for special missions.

Ms. Smith: Special missions for whom?

Teresa: For the government.

Ms. Smith: What type of missions?

TERESA: I don't exactly know. But I remember that he told me that it was very dangerous and he was gone for several months.

MS. SMITH: How many months?

TERESA: About four.

MS. SMITH: Did you and your husband live in the capital for a long time?

TERESA: Not long, just long enough to find a *coyote* to bring us here.

MS. SMITH: And did you manage to get one?

TERESA: Yes.

MS. SMITH: What relatives do you have still in El Salvador?

TERESA: My grandmother, three younger brothers and one younger sister who live with her, and another sister who stayed with an aunt.

MS. SMITH: Have you had any news of them lately?

TERESA: No.

MS. SMITH: How long has it been since you heard from them?

TERESA: We haven't received a letter from any of them for more than six months.

MS. SMITH: Do you have any idea why you haven't heard from them?

TERESA: No, none.

MS. SMITH: How do you feel about that?

TERESA: I feel very bad.

MS. SMITH: Is there anyone to whom you can write to ask about your family?

TERESA: No.

MS. SMITH: Does your husband have family in your country?

TERESA: Yes, his grandmother and an aunt on his mother's side.

MS. SMITH: When did you first find out that you could apply for political asylum in this country?

TERESA: When Immigration arrested me.

MS. SMITH: Did the Immigration officer explain it to you?

TERESA: A little.

MS. SMITH: And when you were traveling, did you have any contact with the authorities in any other country?

TERESA: In Benjamin Hill, Mexico.

MS. SMITH: Okay . . .

JUDGE: Benjamin Hill, is that what she said?

MS. SMITH: Yes, Your Honor, but I know nothing about the place, I'm sorry.

TRIAL ATTORNEY: It's south of Nogales, approximately fifty miles from the border.

MS. SMITH: Your group was detained there the first time. Did the Mexican authorities say anything to you about applying for asylum in Mexico?

TERESA: No.

MS. SMITH: What did they do with you?

TERESA: They deported us.

MS. SMITH: To where?

TERESA: To Guatemala.

MS. SMITH: Did you have any contact with the authorities in Guatemala?

TERESA: No.

MS. SMITH: Then how did you finally come to the United States?

TERESA: We went back to El Salvador, and after a few days we found another *coyote*, who brought us here.

MS. SMITH: About when did this occur?

TERESA: In 1985 also.

MS. SMITH: Teresa, I have just a couple more questions for you, regarding the matter of voluntary departure. Except for having been detained by Immigration authorities, once in Mexico and once here, have you ever been arrested?

TERESA: No.

MS. SMITH: Have you ever committed a crime anywhere in the world?

TERESA: No.

MS. SMITH: If it were necessary, could you pay for your transportation from the United States to El Salvador?

TERESA: Yes.

MS. SMITH: And if there were no other remedy in your case and the judge granted you voluntary departure, would you obey his order?

TERESA: Yes.

MS. SMITH: I have no further questions, Your Honor.

38

On Tuesday, rumors were circulating in the neighborhood that the disturbances would begin at exactly 6 p.m. and that the rioters would disobey the curfew that took effect at 7.

On 16th Street the police lined up and marched. The tension of the authorities, the local residents and the growing number of reporters from national and international news organizations intensified with the passing of the hours and the fall of night on the Adams Morgan district.

This time the police were prepared with greater strength and efficiency to counteract the demonstrators. The television cameras were ready to report live on another night of violence in the nation's capital.

It would have taken only a thrown bottle, like the previous night, to make the fire explode. But, perhaps through some miracle, that bottle was never thrown. The curfew took effect and the riots ended.

The official report summarized the incidents of the two tragic nights:

> As a result of the disturbances, 10 officers were wounded, including one stabbed in the shoulder. Five patrol cars and one police wagon were burned and several other vehicles were damaged by the throwing of rocks and other objects. A large number of private vehicles belonging to area residents were also damaged as a result of the riots. Added to this are the considerable losses caused ⸌ to the 7-Eleven and El Progreso stores in the 3100 block of Mount Pleasant Street, N.W., and one bus completely destroyed between Mount Pleasant and Lamont Streets, N.W. A total of eight arrests were made due to the civil disturbances.

The official report, nevertheless, failed to document the fundamental reasons which generated, and fueled, the two nights of violence. Several local Spanish-language newspapers undertook the task of enumerating them; one of them commented:

> The gunshot that wounded Daniel was only the spark which set off the time bomb that had been waiting to explode in the community due to frustration and discontent for various reasons. One of them is the police mistreatment that our community has suffered repeatedly. Evidence of this has been formally presented to the City of Washington, D.C. by community organizations, and not the least bit of attention has been paid to it. To this, one must add the lack of work training programs. Of maximum importance is the implementation of an acculturation program so the immigrant community can become familiar with the new culture in which it is living. If proper attention is not paid to the situation that this community is suffering, the conflicts will continue to accumulate and will explode again at the least expected moment. As a representative of the city said, "These people, legally documented or not, are here and are a reality that we must take into consideration, and not keep them on the margins of our society. Although they may represent a problem, the city cannot presume to get rid of them as it does its garbage; it cannot pack them up and go dump them somewhere else."

Meanwhile, in a Washington, D.C., hospital, according to newspaper accounts, Daniel "remained in critical but stable condition." And a short time later, luckily for him and perhaps to the benefit of the entire community, he recovered from the gunshot that almost took his life.

39

Under the strict vigilance of guards, the prisoners were taken to a room where an attorney who specialized in immigration matters was waiting for them. She said her name was Susana and she had been sent by a community organization dedicated to helping the undocumented. She explained:

"Each of you had to sign a document in which a date has been set for a hearing, to be held a week after you were first detained. At the hearing, each of you must go before an immigration judge who will decide if you did in fact cross the border without documents. If you deny that allegation, you will later have a hearing in which you will have to prove the date and manner of your entry into this country. If you admit having entered without inspection, the judge will see if there is any alternative to deportation, such as political asylum.

"A bond has been set on each of you. Those who have a bond of five thousand dollars might possibly have it reduced to twenty-five hundred dollars during a bond reduction hearing. But as long as the bond is not paid, you will be held here unless you win your political asylum case.

"As long as there is no final deportation order in your case, you have the right to post bond, be released, and pursue your case while free on bond.

"If you ask for deportation or the judge decides that you should be deported, you will be sent back to your country whenever the Immigration Service has room for you in the seats it pays for on commercial airlines. Your bonds can be posted by your friends or relatives, unless you yourselves have the money to pay it here.

"If you are released on bond, you will leave here with a hearing date pending with the court. At the hearing the judge will determine if in that period of time you obtained an employment letter or managed to achieve some other means of obtaining legal residency. Another option is applying for political asylum, a very special process because it takes a long time and you must prove, through testimony or other evidence, that your life will be in danger if you return to your country.

"If you post bond but then fail to show up for your hearing, which is often held about three months after posting bond, the money that your relatives deposited will be lost and an order will be issued for your arrest and deportation."

After that long explanation, the attorney asked if all of them had understood. No one responded, perhaps because they were still traumatized by their recent capture. She handed each of them a card.

"If you need my help, please call me," added the attorney as she left the room.

The prisoners were escorted back inside El Corralón.

40

Compañero Tzi-Vihán:

The panorama surrounding me now is totally different from the one that surrounded us just a few weeks ago. I am now in the North, at my brother's house. The trip was intense, sad and painful, very tiring and often confusing and even dangerous. The behavior of the guides left much to be desired. One of them tried to rape me. Fortunately someone intervened and stopped him. But then the same man who had defended me tried the same thing. Luckily I knew how to defend myself. The training we received in the mountains served me well on this trip.

This is a different culture, language, people, and land, another world into which I've been thrust and to which I don't know if I will be able to adapt. They say all things are possible, but in my current situation, I have very serious doubts about my adaptation to this country. Nevertheless, I'm determined to try, to make the effort, and, God willing, the time will pass quickly and the war will end so we can be together again. Because being away from you is my greatest suffering, *Compañero* Tzi-Vihán. Nothing, not even the most beautiful spring landscape, is comparable to your love. And that is my greatest grief. Without you, the days are endless, the nights eternal, the world senseless.

I realize all these complaints are truly selfish. Forgive me, *compañero*. Because I understand that when all is said and done, our situation is part of the struggle against social injustice, and I shouldn't complain, because we are fighting for a better world for everyone.

That's why, in my difficult moments, I think of you. I say your name, and then it seems that the world is not completely lost. Take good care of yourself, my love. Please keep writing to me.

"The people will overcome."

Tzu-Nihá

41

(Kitchen. Calixto is busy washing dishes. Juancho, his co-worker,
is scrubbing an enormous aluminum pot
in which the restaurant's soups are made.)

Juancho, hand me the soap.
My name isn't Juancho anymore; now I'm Johnnie.
(*Calixto, surprised.*) Yoni! What kind of name is that?
No, it's not Yoni; it's pronounced Johnnie.
I don't understand! Your name is Juancho Molinos. Knock it off!
It *was*; now it's Johnnie Mills!
What's gotten into you?
You know, when in Rome . . . So now my name is Johnnie.

Hm, this country changes even your name! A waiter that works Saturdays calls me Cal instead of Calixto. I told him *cal* is what we use for painting houses back home. They call it *whitewash* here.

Anyway, don't call me Juancho anymore.

I see you've forgotten the days when you went around barefoot back in the village, with your sack of tortillas on your shoulder.

Yes, but we're not there now.

But that doesn't mean that you're not from there anymore. You can change your name but not your peasant face.

Look what nice shoes I bought. I bet you're jealous.

Just remember when you were barefoot.

That was before. I'm not like all those people who live here but keep thinking they're back there. This is something else! People have to get with the times!

That's true, but I'm not going to forget my town either. How could I ever choose white bread over tortillas? Hamburgers over *pupusas*? Hot dogs over *tamales*? Never! There's no comparison!

Yes, but you haven't forgotten the oxcart either. You still smell like the woods. Not me, I've bought myself a Trans Am!

Sure, and you have to work day and night to pay for it. That's why I prefer to travel on foot, and not have those worries.

I got myself a little *gringa* too. Aw, look at Calixto, he's drooling!

Not me, I have my wife and children, who'll be here soon because I've already saved enough money to pay the *coyote* who's going to bring them. Besides, you don't speak English. You and your girlfriend probably don't even understand each other!

Don't be a fool! We don't have to say a word; we let our hands do the talking!

Yeah, but you need a lot of money, because American women aren't satisfied with just a little, like our women are.

Isn't that what we're here for? To work hard and buy all we want, and be happy? If not, where's the progress and happiness we came here looking for?

You're mixing apples and oranges, Juancho. Getting ahead is one thing; going crazy buying unnecessary things is another. They don't sell happiness in fancy department stores.

I told you my name is Johnnie!

Look, I've known you as Juancho since we were little kids back home, and to me, with or without your car and your *gringuita*, you'll always be Juancho.

But you have to understand that I'm a different person now!

Then, does that mean you're not Salvadoran anymore?

Now I'm from here!

Well, not me. Every day I'm more Salvadoran. Because it's one thing to make progress, have a job, live better, but your home is always in your heart. I could live away from my country for a hundred years but I'll never renounce it.

(*A woman's voice is heard, calling from the doorway of the kitchen.*) Johnnie, honey, are you ready to go?

(*Juancho shouts.*) Yes, I'm coming!

(*To Calixto.*) Gotta go, she's here to pick me up, see you later.

(*She enters the kitchen and, before leaving with Juancho, says goodbye to Calixto.*) Goodbye, Cal!

(*Calixto, in Spanish.*) My name's not Cal, it's Calixto!
(*She, not understanding, smiles and repeats.*) Goodbye, Cal!
(*Calixto, annoyed.*) *Adiós.*

42

At 6 a.m. the alarm went off in El Corralón. The prisoners woke from their fitful sleep and headed toward the open-air bathrooms to wash up.

At 7 a.m. the bell was heard again, this time to signal that it was time for breakfast. The prisoners got in line and went into the kitchen, took a tray and were served the food they wanted. The food was not bad, and they were given half an hour to eat. Five minutes before breakfast ended those who were still hungry were permitted to have seconds.

At 7:30 everyone had to go out onto the soccer field; no one was permitted to stay in the dining rooms or sleeping areas. The prison also had a tennis court, but the inmates were only provided balls for the game of soccer. In a small building that they called the Casino, there were cards and board games for the entertainment of the detainees.

They would stay on the field and in the Casino until noon, when the alarm sounded to indicate lunch, after which they would return to the yard, where they would stay until 6 p.m., when supper was served. By 6:30 everyone had eaten and returned to the huge dormitory areas filled with cots, with a color television in each corner.

For most of the prisoners, men and women, this was the first time they had seen a color television, since many of them had never left their remote villages before their trip to the United States. Therefore they spent long hours in front of the television, as if hypnotized even by the commercials.

At 10 p.m. the lights and televisions were turned off, except for a few lights in the corridors leading to the yard. From that time on, talking out loud was prohibited.

Such was the daily routine in El Corralón.

When the detainees entered the prison, their personal belong-ings, such as watches and other jewelry, were taken from them. If they had any money in their possession, they were permitted to keep only five dollars inside the prison. The rest was kept in an envelope to be returned to them at the time of their release.

The five dollars were given to the inmates in quarters; with them they could purchase candy bars, peanuts, chewing gum, cigarettes and sodas from a machine which was refilled every Thursday. When the five dollars were gone and the prisoners wanted more money, they had the option of earning a dollar a day working in the kitchen, cleaning the building, or serving as messengers for the officers. Those who worked were known as "handymen."

No one knew how long they would have to remain in the prison. Their length of stay depended on many factors: the attorneys, the money their relatives had available for bond, and luck.

43

JUDGE: Mr. Hammer, do you have questions for the Respondent?

TRIAL ATTORNEY: Yes, Your Honor, thank you . . . Teresa, have you ever used any other name?

TERESA: No.

TRIAL ATTORNEY: The only times you've been arrested or detained were by the Mexican and United States Immigration authorities, is that correct?

TERESA: Yes.

TRIAL ATTORNEY: I suppose, then, that you've never been in jail.

TERESA: No.

TRIAL ATTORNEY: I'm a little confused about some dates. Your applications says that you were born in 1960. When was it that you lived with your grandmother?

TERESA: Since my parents died.

TRIAL ATTORNEY: And when was that?

TERESA: My father has been dead for twelve years. My mother died thirteen years ago.

TRIAL ATTORNEY: Well, did you live with your grandmother until the time you left your country?

TERESA: When I went to live with my husband, then I lived separately from her.

TRIAL ATTORNEY: And approximately when was that?

TERESA: In 1976.

TRIAL ATTORNEY: After 1976 you no longer lived with your grandmother?

TERESA: Not with her, no, but we lived nearby.

TRIAL ATTORNEY: In how many different places did you live with your husband?

TERESA: Just there where we had our house and in San Miguel. And about a month in the capital.

TRIAL ATTORNEY: How far is San Miguel from where your grandmother lived?

TERESA: By bus, it takes an hour.

JUDGE: Do me a favor, Mr. Hammer, and ask her the name of the city where the grandmother lived.

TRIAL ATTORNEY: In what city or village did your grandmother live?

TERESA: Cantón el Jocote, San Miguel.

JUDGE: Thank you.

TRIAL ATTORNEY: The only contact you had with the guerrillas was when they would come to your house and your grandmother's house for water?

TERESA: I talked to them two or three times when they came to ask for water. After that they would just come and take the water themselves from the barrel that was there.

TRIAL ATTORNEY: I don't understand your answer. You say that you talked with them two or three times?

TERESA: Yes, when they asked us if we had water.

TRIAL ATTORNEY: Well, how often did you see the guerrillas in the area, once a day, once a month, once a year?

TERESA: Once a week, but they would pass through there every night.

TRIAL ATTORNEY: How often would you see the military in that area, once a day, once a month, once a year?

TERESA: The soldiers were always there every day, checking the buses, looking for guerrillas.

TRIAL ATTORNEY: Did you ever have any problems with the military?

TERESA: No.

TRIAL ATTORNEY: Did you have any problems with any other official of the Salvadoran government?

TERESA: No.

JUDGE: Was your husband forcibly recruited into the military, or did he volunteer?

TERESA: He volunteered.

TRIAL ATTORNEY: And he signed up for how long?

TERESA: In San Miguel, he was in for about a year and a half. In San Salvador, four months. Here in the United States, I don't remember if it was three or four months.

TRIAL ATTORNEY: You say that he entered the service voluntarily. Did he volunteer to serve a year or two years or ten years? For how long did he sign up?

TERESA: When he went in the first time in San Miguel, he was only there four months and then they brought him here. After he returned from the United States, he was always in combat.

TRIAL ATTORNEY: How long did the rules say he had to stay in the army?

TERESA: Two years.

TRIAL ATTORNEY: So your husband was supposed to get out of the army in 1984?

TERESA: No, because the four months that he was here didn't count.

TRIAL ATTORNEY: When was it that the guerrillas detained your husband?

JUDGE: Excuse me, and in what year?

TERESA: In 1984.

TRIAL ATTORNEY: January or December? June?

TERESA: I don't remember.

TRIAL ATTORNEY: Well, after he deserted the army, you and he moved to another city, San Miguel?

TERESA: Yes.

TRIAL ATTORNEY: How long did you live in San Miguel before you left the country?

TERESA: Two, three, four months.

TRIAL ATTORNEY: Okay now, your application says that you left El Salvador in January of 1985. Was that the only time you left your country?

TERESA: No, twice in 1985.

TRIAL ATTORNEY: When the Mexican authorities detained you, they didn't return you to your country?

TERESA: No, they sent us to Guatemala.

TRIAL ATTORNEY: They just left you on the other side of the border?

TERESA: We crossed the border into Guatemala and they kept us in a place that was like a jail for three or four days. Then they let us go and we returned to El Salvador.

TRIAL ATTORNEY: Okay. After your husband deserted the army, did he have any further problems with the guerrillas?

TERESA: No.

TRIAL ATTORNEY: When you moved from the small village to San Miguel, did that diminish the amount of combat in the area?

TERESA: No.

TRIAL ATTORNEY: And if you had moved to the capital, in your experience, is there less combat there?

TERESA: No.

TRIAL ATTORNEY: Where did you get your passport?

TERESA: In the capital.

TRIAL ATTORNEY: When was that?

TERESA: When we lived there for about a month.

TRIAL ATTORNEY: Hm . . . Let's move to another subject. Did you receive a passport issued by the government of El Salvador?

TERESA: Yes.

TRIAL ATTORNEY: You got it before leaving the country?

TERESA: Yes.

TRIAL ATTORNEY: And you obtained it in the capital?

TERESA: Yes, that's where we got our passports.

TRIAL ATTORNEY: You got it in the capital.

TERESA: Yes.

TRIAL ATTORNEY: Fine, fine. Then, you and your husband, both of you, obtained passports before leaving El Salvador?

TERESA: Yes, sir.

TRIAL ATTORNEY: And then you and he left by bus, plane? How did you leave?

TERESA: By bus.

TRIAL ATTORNEY: And you said that you had gotten a visa. Did you have a visa to go to Mexico?

TERESA: Yes.

TRIAL ATTORNEY: You received a visa for Mexico at the time you got your passports?

TERESA: Yes.

TRIAL ATTORNEY: And did you get a visa for the United States?

TERESA: No.

TRIAL ATTORNEY: Why not?

TERESA: We didn't try to get one, because my husband was fleeing and, besides, it was too complicated because we couldn't meet the requirements.

TRIAL ATTORNEY: Hm . . . Has your husband always used the same name?

TERESA: No.

TRIAL ATTORNEY: So you obtained your passport with your true name and he with a false name?

TERESA: He had to use a false name because he was afraid they would discover that he had deserted from the army.

TRIAL ATTORNEY: And did you travel together?

TERESA: Yes. But during the trip we didn't talk to each other.

TRIAL ATTORNEY: Hm . . . Why?

TERESA: So no one would suspect we were husband and wife. That way, if the authorities discovered and arrested him, they wouldn't arrest me.

44

FOR A FEW DAYS, MOUNT PLEASANT
OPENED A WINDOW TO THE WORLD

The looting, violence and clashes with police captured first the attention of the national, then the world news media. Sunday night, after midnight, the scenes of riots in Mount Pleasant presented vivid images on the world and national news network CNN. Burned patrol cars and police vans provided the footage for CNN's lead story early Monday morning.

By Monday, with the violence and looting at their height, one could observe the large gathering of reporters from world news agencies forming part of the press deployed throughout the area. Representatives of Canada, Korea, England, Spain and France, to mention just a few, joined forces with the local and national media.

Correspondents from *El Tiempo Latino* in Buenos Aires, Argentina, mentioned the attention the story of the riots received in the press of that country, noting that film footage was seen on news programs, and photos of the looting appeared in newspapers there.

A continuing concern on Tuesday, when the curfew was set to go into effect at 7 p.m., was that the number of reporters focusing their cameras on the police and the crowd could incite a riot. The effect of attracting attention was sufficient to precipitate a confrontation. For example, the Israelis allege that the international television cameras installed in the occupied territories instigated the Palestinians to throw stones during the tragic Intifada.

Nevertheless, it did not happen like that in this case. The relative lack of violence on Tuesday was a relief (although some said it was a disappointment for the reporters who had just arrived for that third night).

In the first place, it was unclear whether the curfew included reporters. The police apparently wanted to establish a system of news groups (such as what was used for coverage of the Gulf War). The complaint by Len Downie, editor of the *Washington Post*, changed all that. In fact, this influential local newspaper deployed a large number of reporters and photographers, providing coverage of a part of the community that is usually filed away and forgotten. The *Washington Times* also had its people well installed. Other media, among the many, were *The New York Times* (which put the story on the first page on Tuesday), the *Baltimore Sun* and almost all the news agencies.

Journalists, in general, enjoyed freedom of movement. Some police officers were open with us, pausing during breaks in the action to offer their observations about the situation.

A joke going around among the reporters was that the Washington, D.C. police had lost more vehicles in the two days of violence than the U.S. military lost in its entire operation against Iraq.

El Tiempo Latino
Washington, D.C.
May 10, 1991

45

Silvia, Elisa and the other women captured with Calixto's group were also being held at El Corralón. The two young women who had been separated from the group by the guides, to cross the border with them, were there also. They had developed a relationship of trust with Elisa and Silvia, to whom they related what had happened.

"The guides took us to a dark place and raped us," said one of them. "They threatened that if we refused, they wouldn't help us cross the border and they would abandon us."

The other added, "But after they abused us, they abandoned us there in the darkness of the desert. We walked about an hour and a half until we found a river and managed to cross it."

"But once we were on the other side of the river," said the first, "the police captured us and turned us over to Immigration. That's how we ended up here."

"I had an even worse experience," said an eighteen-year-old girl who had made friends with Silvia. "Back home, my parents were killed in the crossfire during a battle between the guerrillas and the army. Since I was an orphan and had nowhere to live, my uncle paid seven hundred dollars to a *coyote* who was bringing a group to take me to an aunt who lives in Los Angeles. The trip went fine. We crossed the border and then stayed a few days in a city near the border. The *coyote* went out one day to buy food and never came back; maybe they arrested him. Anyway, our group of thirty people was left abandoned in that hotel. And no one knew what to do. I got so desperate after going hungry for three days that I went out to look for the guide or get help. A policeman who spoke Spanish stopped me and, when he found out that I was undocumented, offered me a job as a maid in his house. He seemed really nice, and I accepted. I ironed, cooked and cleaned for him, but he never paid me a cent. He raped me many times and slept with me as if I were his wife. He threatened to kill me if I told anyone. I told him I wanted to go to school to learn English, but he told me that people without papers had no right to anything. I lived a year and a half in that life of slavery, until one time when the policeman had to travel out of town for a few days, I escaped and was headed to Los Angeles to find my aunt. But I had such bad luck that the *migra* caught me at the bus station, and that's how I ended up here. Now I'm just waiting to be deported."

46

(*Kitchen. Calixto, Cali, Caremacho, Juancho, Chele Chile.*)

November second is a date that's firmly etched on my mind.

Why's that?

That's when we celebrate the Day of the Dead in my country.

But the truth is there's not a special day for remembering the dead there anymore, since now there are dead and disappeared people every day of the year.

That day reminds me of La Bermeja.

What's La Bermeja?

The poor people's cemetery, where the crosses are made of dry branches and where those who can't afford a gravesite bury their dead in other people's graves.

So people sometimes take flowers to the wrong grave.

That's right. There's no comparison between La Bermeja and the elegant General Cemetery, Los Ilustres.

Where are those located?

In the capital too. That's where the rich people of the country are buried, in mausoleums that look like marble castles, decorated with statues of angels and saints.

But it doesn't matter how or where the dead are buried. Everything ends there.

There are no more words to say.

A friend of mine disappeared mysteriously. One morning he went out to go to work and he never came back. His wife asked me to help her find him.

Where did you look for him?

Everywhere. We went to the National Police, the Treasury Police, the National Guard, all the military bases, and no one knew anything about him.

Did you ever find him?

Finally, in a morgue, we managed to identify his body. They had cut off one of his arms. In La Bermeja we were told that there was no room to bury him, that there were so many dead bodies that they didn't even fit in the cemetery anymore.

So where did you bury him?

We had to pay a bribe to one of the gravediggers. That's the only way we could bury him in the cemetery.

So what do people who don't have any money do? What do they do with their dead?

The bodies accumulate in the morgues. Finally they throw them into big pits and burn them.

That's what they did with the Jews in the concentration camps.

The poor people don't even have enough money to bury their dead according to God's commands.

That's why whenever I remember the Day of the Dead, I feel so sad. It's not a day that brings me pleasant memories.

I remember the sweet pastries with honey they make for that day. They're delicious.

I always think of the beautiful wreaths of flowers people put on the graves of their loved ones.

I also recall the poor children who steal the flowers and then sell them at the entrance to the cemetery.

I remember the old women who carry pictures of their dead relatives to the cemetery to put on the graves while they mourn.

I saw all that too. But, on the Day of the Dead, I picture my country as one enormous cemetery.

47

The detainees wore U. S. Army pants and jackets, especially in the winter, since they did not have appropriate clothing for the cold weather. The jackets had labels bearing the names of their former owners, and the prisoners would jokingly call each other by those last names. It sounded comical to them to call a Mexican, Peruvian, Guatemalan or companion with indigenous features Smith, McDonald, or Peterson. The last names, most of them Irish, Scandinavian or Polish, such as Joyce, Hutchinson and Kosikowski, were impossible for them to pronounce.

The first time Calixto and the soldier went out to walk around the soccer field, they were immediately told who the leader of one of the groups that controlled the jail was: a Cuban called Marielón, a short, muscular man.

Calixto and the soldier headed for the Casino, which was next to the officers' bathroom; for security reasons it was the only bathroom in the whole prison with a mirror. The strict security regulations also prohibited knives and forks, even in the dining room. At mealtimes each prisoner was given a spoon, which had to be returned upon leaving the dining room; otherwise the prisoner was not permitted to leave and was isolated from the others in a special cell, because the spoon could be sharpened and used as a weapon with which to escape, as one prisoner had done some time before.

Calixto and the soldier noticed as Marielón approached a Mexican and said, "Listen man, I'll take care of your money, give me the five dollars and don't worry. I'll make sure nothing happens to it."

The Mexican refused and a member of Marielón's gang knocked him to the ground. Three guards saw how the man was assaulted, but they did not intervene. Some other Mexicans were witnesses to the attack also, but did not defend their fellow countryman who, after being beaten and kicked, lay unconscious on the dusty field.

Marielón stole the man's money and proceeded calmly to the canteen, where he bought cigarettes and candy bars. The guards called the infirmary to come and pick up the wounded man.

From then on, most of the prisoners chose to hand over their money when Marielón asked for it, to avoid problems with his frightening gang.

Calixto and the soldier were near the officers' bathroom, which at that moment was being cleaned by some prisoners. They saw that the door of the Casino was open and they went in. Two men were sitting at a table playing chess, surrounded by several onlookers who were watching attentively. Although many of them did not understand the game, it seemed interesting to them, especially because of the shapes of the pieces. At other tables inmates were playing cards, dominoes and checkers, but no one was watching them because those were common, boring games; chess, on the other hand, they considered new and different.

Calixto and the soldier walked among the tables, listened to the conversations and then went back out to the field. Calixto saw the handymen cleaning the officers' bathroom and noticed that it had a mirror.

Several uniformed officers, equipped with pistols and radio transmitters, guarded the area, which was also under camera surveillance.

Over the loudspeakers located at the corners of the field and at several other points within the prison, the usual messages were announced: "Eulalio Pérez, report to the office; you have a call from your relatives in Houston!"

The prisoner's friends were happy for him and congratulated him, slapping him on the back and shaking his hand, since perhaps this was the telephone call that held the key to his release.

Marielón's gang had attacked the Mexican at 10:30 that morning, and by noon they were again stealing money from all the Mexicans they could find, whom they had already identified, especially a group from Zacatecas to which their first victim belonged. About twenty-five of them had been captured at the border. They had left their country driven by their desire to work and make enough money to support their families.

For the most part the prisoners were peasants from different parts of Mexico, Central and South America and the Caribbean. Strangely, in El Corralón, there were also detainees from India, Vietnam and Korea. All the inmates, regardless of their origin, had tragic personal stories. Once they were travelers in a caravan undertaking a dramatic odyssey toward the vast lands of the North; now they were shipwrecked survivors of a boat that sank in the Río Grande while crossing the border.

Marielón, followed by his henchmen, approached Calixto and said, "Hey you, buy me a Coke."

"Sure, anything you say," said Calixto, handing him two quarters. "I don't want to have problems with anybody."

The bully smiled maliciously, took the coins, and walked away. Ten minutes later he returned and said to Calixto, "Hey, be careful. It's dangerous to have money on you in this place. Why don't you give it to me and I'll take care of it for you?"

The gang members surrounded Calixto, who decided that the best thing was to hand over the money to avoid trouble. "Anyway," he said to himself, "I don't smoke and I don't need to drink Coke."

Just when Calixto was putting his hand into his pocket to get out the money, someone shoved him hard from behind, causing him to fall to the ground, burying his jaw in the dust of the yard. Someone else then kicked him in the leg.

Calixto managed to get up and rush toward the officers' bathroom, which was about ten yards away. With his elbow protected by the thick sleeve of the army jacket, he broke the mirror, grabbed a piece of glass about five inches long and crouched down in the dark interior of the room, against a wall near the doorway, to wait.

When Marielón, announced by the dry tapping of the heels of his army boots, entered, Calixto, blindly and without looking for a certain target, stabbed at him, slicing his face from the chin, through the lips, nose and one eye. Marielón retreated, falling backward onto the steps at the entrance to the bathroom. He rolled down into the dirt yard, screaming in pain and covering his face.

Immediately, several of the prisoners in the area, who had been intently watching the clash, fell on Marielón, kicking and punching him. The members of his gang attempted to counter the attack in defense of their leader, but the group from Zacatecas threw themselves into the fray to avenge the dishonor suffered by their compatriot.

When the guards arrived to restore order, some of Marielón's henchmen took off running. Calixto dropped the piece of glass and left the area, followed by the soldier. He stopped at the opposite side of the field to observe from a distance the commotion that had been created by the fight.

Meanwhile, several members of Marielón's gang lay unconscious in the dust, near their leader, who was bleeding profusely.

48

Compañera Tzu-Nihá:

I write you on behalf of *compañero* Tzi-Vihán, that is, in memory of him, because our *compañero* is now a hero who fell in the struggle on behalf of our people. I fought at his side to the end of the difficult mission, and I can tell you that he died like the great ones, fighting, rifle in hand, giving not an inch to the enemy, shouting battle orders and saying the names of our heroes of the past and, I'm sure, thinking of your love.

Compañero Tzi-Vihán was buried with all the honors reserved for heroes. When I die, I hope to do so as he did, head high, confronting the enemy, spilling my blood for the sake of our oppressed and dispossessed people. Here are the words of the song that we sang at his funeral:

> Ask me not who I am
> or if we've ever met,
> the dreams I had
> will exist though I am gone,
> I no longer live but I do go on
> in what I was dreaming
> Those who keep fighting
> will make new roses grow
> And in the name of those roses
> You will all remember me.
> Recall not my face
> for my face was of war
> as long as there was in my land

the need for me to hate,
in the sky that's already clearing
you will know my true face.
Few people ever heard me laugh
but my laugh you never knew
will be found in the dawn
of the coming day.
Ask not my age,
my age is that of everyone.
I chose in many ways
to be older than my age,
and my true years
were the shots from my gun.
I am born again in each one,
and although my body may die
I will be the true age
of the child I have liberated.
Seek not my grave
because you will not find it.
My hands are those that go on
in other hands that are shooting,
my voice the one that is shouting,
my dream the one that is still intact,
and know that I will only die
if you give in
because those who die fighting
live on in every *compañero*.

49

TRIAL ATTORNEY: Hm . . . And you left your country by bus?

TERESA: Yes.

TRIAL ATTORNEY: Did you work in El Salvador?

TERESA: Yes.

TRIAL ATTORNEY: What kind of work did you do and approximately what were you paid?

TERESA: I worked in the fields, hoeing and picking during harvest time.

TRIAL ATTORNEY: How much did you earn per day or per week?

TERESA: Five *colones* a day.

TRIAL ATTORNEY: Do you know how much that would be in dollars?

TERESA: About a dollar.

TRIAL ATTORNEY: Your application says that apparently one of the reasons for which you left or one of your problems was that work was very uncertain from one day to the next in your country. Is that true?

TERESA: No, the real reason was because of the help we gave the guerrillas, which puts me in danger if I go back.

TRIAL ATTORNEY: Well, is the declaration on your application true or false?

TERESA: It's true. There isn't a lot of work. When you work there, it's just for food, that's all, but that's not the reason I left. My life is in danger if I go back to my country, because I helped the guerrillas.

TRIAL ATTORNEY: In the area where you lived, didn't the guerrillas take water whenever they wanted to?

TERESA: No, it was a well, and if they didn't have a pail to put down into the well to get the water, they couldn't do it, so they would take barrels or pails that we had around that they could get. That was the only way they could do it.

TRIAL ATTORNEY: Okay, did the well belong to your grandmother, or was it a community well?

TERESA: It was about three kilometers from the village where we lived.

TRIAL ATTORNEY: So the water the guerrillas took was water that you and other people in the area had carried from the community well.

TERESA: That's right.

TRIAL ATTORNEY: Have you worked in this country?

TERESA: Yes.

TRIAL ATTORNEY: What type of work?

TERESA: Cleaning offices.

JUDGE: How much do you earn per day?

TERESA: $3.35 was what they paid me.

TRIAL ATTORNEY: Per hour or per day?

TERESA: Per hour.

TRIAL ATTORNEY: Did you know that it was illegal to enter this country without inspection?

TERESA: Yes.

TRIAL ATTORNEY: So that is the only crime you have committed?

TERESA: Yes.

TRIAL ATTORNEY: Your grandmother, or your husband's grandparents, have they been arrested or have they had any problems with the military?

TERESA: No, I don't know.

TRIAL ATTORNEY: Have they had any problems with the guerrillas, other than that they would take the water?

TERESA: No, I don't know.

TRIAL ATTORNEY: To be sure that I've understood, I understood you to say that your husband had deserted the military service instead of resigning. Did I understand you correctly?

TERESA: He left because he was threatened, because they threatened him; otherwise he would not have left.

TRIAL ATTORNEY: Fine, but he never asked the army's permission to abandon his military service?

TERESA: No.

TRIAL ATTORNEY: So you believe that as far as the army knows, he's dead?

TERESA: Yes, sir.

JUDGE: Mr. Hammer, I'm going to interrupt you now too. I simply don't want to hear any more about this husband. I think that has been covered sufficiently. The only intelligent question that I wanted to ask, which I will give to you, is what's this guy's name?

TRIAL ATTORNEY: What is your husband's name?

TERESA: Secenio González.

TRIAL ATTORNEY: How do you spell that?

TERESA: How do you spell Secenio?

TRIAL ATTORNEY: Yes.

TERESA: I don't know. I don't know how to read or write.

TRIAL ATTORNEY: First "s" and then "c," or first "c" and then "s"?

TERESA: "S" and then "c," I think.

TRIAL ATTORNEY: I understand from your application that you have never been a member of any organization here or anywhere else?

TERESA: I don't understand the question.

TRIAL ATTORNEY: Were you ever a member of any organization, like a club, society, union, or political party?

TERESA: No.

TRIAL ATTORNEY: Did you enter this country with the help of a *coyote* or in some other way?

TERESA: With a *coyote*.

TRIAL ATTORNEY: From your testimony, it would appear that conditions in your country are dangerous. Is that a fair summary?

TERESA: Yes.

TRIAL ATTORNEY: And it appears that many people are in very difficult situations, isn't that right?

TERESA: Yes.

TRIAL ATTORNEY: You have testified that if you had to leave this country, you would. Where would you go?

TERESA: I wouldn't like to go anywhere, but I will obey the judge's order.

TRIAL ATTORNEY: I have no further questions, Your Honor.

JUDGE: Ms. Smith, do you have any further questions for the respondent?

Ms. SMITH: I believe I have just one more question . . . Teresa, do you know how many more months your husband had left to serve in the army when he left?

TERESA: I think eight months, but I'm not too sure.

Ms. SMITH: No further questions, Your Honor.

JUDGE: Thank you, Teresa: you may step down. Ms. Smith, do you have further witnesses or evidence?

Ms. SMITH: No, Your Honor.

JUDGE: Mr. Hammer?

TRIAL ATTORNEY: No further witnesses or evidence, Your Honor.

50

(Kitchen. Calixto, Cali, Caremacho, Juancho, Chele Chile.)

Last night I was at Don Chencho's house.

The healer?

That's the one.

What did you go there for? That old guy is a witch doctor!

No way! You should see how he cures people. One of my wife's cousins hurt her foot at work and it got real swollen.

They should have gone to the hospital.

No, the people at the hospital ask more questions than a priest at confession. They make you wait for hours and hours and then they don't give you even so much as an aspirin.

That's for sure. A friend of mine had an accident and they took him to the hospital, and the doctors refused to take care of him because he didn't have insurance. He lost so much blood that the poor guy ended up all anemic.

(Chele Chile, sadly.) The hospitals here are a disaster.

That's why my wife's cousin chose to go to Don Chencho. And he massaged her leg, and the swelling went down, and the next day she could walk with no pain; she didn't miss even one day of work!

And how much did he charge her?

Fifteen dollars.

A doctor would have charged at least fifty. And done some complicated treatment.

And would have told her she couldn't work for a week.

And then she would have really been in trouble, because the place where she works doesn't have medical benefits, and anyone who misses, even if they're sick, doesn't get paid.

But why did you go to the healer, Calixto? Are you sick?

Not me. A woman who lives at my cousin's house has a lot of back pain, and she asked me to go with her. She's gone to a lot of doctors, but they just give her expensive pills that don't help her at all.

What did the healer do for her?

Well, first he gave her a massage. Then he gave her a liquid he makes and told her to drink it after eating–a green liquid.

Was it rue water?

Who knows? But one thing's for sure: the woman has faith that it's going to cure her pain.

A friend told me about a man who went to the hospital and they found a rotted worm in his brain. They took him to the healer, who said he had only a few days to live.

What treatment did Don Chencho give him?

He said he couldn't do anything for him here, but that if he were back home he could cure him, because over there he had all the herbs he needed.

People come from everywhere to visit the healer, even from as far away as New York!

He used to live in Maryland. And so many people would go to see him that they didn't all fit in his house. But they say that the doctors in the neighborhood were jealous because people didn't go to them, with all their diplomas and degrees, but rather to a humble man who didn't even speak English. So they reported him and the police arrested him.

Did they put him in jail?

They let him go on the condition that he wouldn't cure people anymore, because in this country only doctors are licensed to do that.

So what happened to Don Chencho?

He came to Washington. And the people have followed him over here; he now has more patients than ever. People have faith in him and are cured.

Some say he's a witch doctor, and that he's made a deal with the devil. But Don Chencho says he simply has a gift from God who has put him here to help poor people who, far from their homes and their customs, are suffering and don't have the time or money to go to doctors who don't understand their language or their illnesses.

51

Thursday was the day the vending machines of soda, cigarettes and candy in El Corralón were filled. That was the same day that a doctor and nurse visited the prison, ordinarily the only opportunity for sick prisoners to get medical attention. But this time, since it was an emergency, an ambulance was called to take Marielón and nine of his cohorts to the hospital.

According to the guards' investigation of the incident, the perpetrators were Calixto, the soldier, three Mexicans, and some other Salvadorans, all of whom were locked up in a cell known as La Loba, a small windowless room with only one door that had a tiny barred opening through which food was given to the detainees.

La Loba was built of concrete blocks, painted a pale yellow color. Inside it was damp, dark and foul smelling. An old wooden bench was the only furniture. The toilet was open, located in one corner, and there the prisoners used it in sight of the others.

One of the Mexicans commented, "Last week a Dominican who was beaten up by Marielón's gang died right here in this cell."

"Yes," affirmed another, "he had been complaining about the abuse he was suffering, but the guards didn't pay any attention to him."

"No one would listen to him."

"Until finally one day they beat him up real bad. And to isolate him from them, the guards decided to put him here in La Loba, where he died."

Calixto and company were locked in that cell for two days; then they were taken before a judge, who declared that the offense committed warranted misdemeanor charges, and that they had the right to have a lawyer. The court assigned them an attorney who, without mincing words, explained the situation to them: "If the bond they've set on you isn't paid within the time set by the judge at your first hearing, after you were caught crossing the border, you'll be sent to a state court and certainly be sentenced to a year and a half in a regular jail, where you'll be detained with true criminals. So it's in your best interest to pressure your friends and relatives to post your bond as soon as possible."

52

A MILLION SALVADORANS
IN THE UNITED STATES

One fifth of El Salvador's population lives in the United States, according to a study carried out by sociologist Segundo Montes of El Salvador's Universidad Centroamericana José Simeón Cañas. The study also revealed that Salvadorans living in the U.S. send more than a billion dollars a year to their relatives back home.

This represents the most extensive analysis to date of the Salvadoran migration to the United States. The study is based on surveys done in 1986 and 1987 of 2,000 families in El Salvador and 1,300 who reside in the U.S., interviewed at embassies and community organizations. It is estimated that between 80,000 and 150,000 Salvadorans live in the Washington, D.C. area, the second highest concentration after Los Angeles.

According to the study, Salvadorans send home an average of $113 per month, a total of 1.3 billion dollars per year, which represents one of the three largest sources of income for this country, the other two being economic aid from the U.S. and earnings from coffee exports.

For the most part the remittances are channeled through unofficial transfer houses, which are beyond the control of Salvadoran banks. The money is primarily invested in housing, food and general consumer goods.

The study confirms that the funds sent by the Salvadorans keep our country's economy afloat. The data also establish that three-fourths of the Salvadorans presently residing in the U.S. arrived after 1979, when the civil war intensified. Almost half, 48.8 percent, arrived after January, 1982.

The analysis also attempted to determine the reasons for the Salvadoran exodus. According to the surveys, 36 percent of those who emigrated after 1980 did so for economic reasons, 28.5 percent for political reasons, and 20 percent for both reasons.

The study also found that 46 percent of those surveyed hope to return home eventually, while 54 percent hope to legalize their residence in the United States.

La Tribuna
San Salvador
June 4, 1988

53

(Kitchen. Calixto, Chele Chile, Cali, Juancho, Caremacho.)

This cold weather makes you wear so many clothes! Back in my home town, I'd go around without a shirt on, and barefoot. The only thing I never went without was my machete, my constant companion.

You never went anywhere without your machete? Why was that?

Because in my town, it's better to be barefoot and shirtless than to be without your machete. Without it I felt completely naked, exposed to any kind of danger.

So what do you do now? You can't carry a machete around in this country.

I wanted to bring it, but the circumstances of my trip made it impossible.

Buy yourself one for Christmas. I know of a store here in Washington that sells them.

The Christmas presents that worry me are the ones for my family. I'm planning to send my wife a pair of shoes, and toys for my kids, but to do that I'm going to have to get a par-tie.

(Cali, intrigued.) What's a "par-tie?"

An extra job, or half-time job.

Oh, you mean part-time.

Yes.

Okay, Calixto, so you already know what you're going to get your family for Christmas. Now all you have to do is find an extra job to get the money.

The kids here want those toys they advertise day and night on television, like pistols, rifles, tanks, boats and war planes. They're expensive.

They're modern toys, not like the ones we had when we were young.

The ones I had, even though they were simple and cheap, were real toys.

I was really happy with my little wooden horse.

The toy I remember most was a wooden alligator, one of those colorful ones you pull with a string and the tail moves back and forth.

Things sure have changed. Nowadays the toys are exact replicas of complicated war armaments.

In my town people go crazy celebrating Christmas and New Year's.

The kids have fun setting off all kinds of fireworks.

The men get drunk. And the women impress everyone preparing their Christmas dinners.

And there's Midnight Mass.

And the climate is pleasant, not like here where it's so cold and you have to be locked up inside right on Christmas Day.

And the poor people who don't have any money for celebrating, what do they do?

In my town everybody was poor, but even if we had to borrow, we'd make an elaborate Nativity scene.

It's like the whole country agrees to put aside its problems and call a truce for Christmas. The radios play the usual songs, like that one that goes,

> Bells are ringing
> Merry Christmas singing,
> sweet memories are heard
> of the blessed home where I was raised,
> Christmas, Christmas.
> And how sad it is to wander in life
> far from home, through lost lands,
> and hear a loving voice
> saying warmly, "Christmas has come."

But sometimes, while everyone was enjoying the Christmas festivities, my family was going through terrible problems, since I didn't have a job and there was no money to buy my children even so much as a little wooden car. That's why, now that I can, I'm going to send them some nice toys so they can have fun.

54

José managed to get in touch with Toño, who by then was residing in Washington, D.C. and promised to lend him the money to pay his bond. When he told several of his fellow prisoners the news that he would soon be released, many of them immediately wrote letters, begging him to contact their relatives as soon as he left El Corralón.

Direct information about who was leaving the jail was provided by the metallic voice from the loudspeakers which, often on the most unexpected day, would surprise an inmate and announce, "Cayetano Martínez, report to the office!" This would set off a round of congratulations and, in a matter of seconds, many inmates would hastily write down names and telephone numbers which they would give to the one who was leaving, entrusting to him all their hopes of being released. This was at times the only possibility that the friends and relatives of a detainee would find out he was in that jail.

All kinds of stories were heard in El Corralón, some simple and others incredible. Prisoners got to know all the details of each other's lives.

The inmates who suffered a lack of communication were those who did not speak Spanish, such as the ones from Jamaica, Haiti, China, India, Korea and Vietnam. Many languages were spoken at El Corralón, but Spanish predominated.

One former smuggler explained to Calixto that the entry route of undocumented Indians was through Canada and New York. But some prisoners commented that they had seen large numbers of Indians and Chinese in Guatemala, who were likely disembarking at Central American ports and then continuing on to Mexico. Others insisted that usually undocumented Indians traveled from India to England, and then from England to Canada or New York.

The presence of prisoners of diverse origins and languages attested to the fact that men and women from the most remote corners of the planet, including Korea, India and China, were finding a way to reach and enter the United States.

One of the most popular characters was Charro, a Mexican who swore that life could not teach him anything new. He had crossed the border at every possible point, known and unknown. He liked to say, "Now I'm a prisoner, poor and miserable, but five years from now I'll be a millionaire. I just have to get out of this damned place. This is just a passing situation of bad luck."

He would give his card to all the detainees and say, very seriously, "When you get out of jail, look me up. I'm at your service, for anything you need."

Charro gave advice, which everyone heeded, as they considered him the detainee with the most experience in the difficult situation of being a wandering and undocumented citizen.

Another notorious character was Turk, a real wheeler-dealer. He always knew exactly who were the prisoners who had come in each day. At night, when it was time for them to go to bed, he would offer his services, asking, "Would you like me to get you a pillow? An extra blanket?"

He would then go through the room and, noticing someone already asleep, would carefully take a pillow or a blanket, until he completed the order, for which he then charged two dollars. He could get anything: soap, toothpaste . . . "If you want a job, I can get you one," he would offer.

Charro and Turk were close friends; they were always the last ones to finish eating and go to bed. When the bell rang at mealtimes, the other prisoners would fight over the places at the front of the line, but Charro and Turk would go to the end of the line and, smoking calmly, they would shout, "Those pigs!"

They knew very well that, no matter one's place in line, there was enough food for everyone. They had been there longer than anyone. No one knew, nor did they reveal, the reason for their detention. But most people said they were there for smuggling undocumented people.

55

JUDGE: The respondent is a twenty-year-old native and citizen of El Salvador who in February of this year was apprehended by agents of the Immigration and Naturalization Service shortly after having entered the United States without inspection.

On that same date, an Order to Show Cause was issued charging deportability under section 241(a)(2) of the Immigration and Nationality Act.

The respondent submitted an application for asylum on form I-589 to request relief from deportation under sections 208(a) and 243(h) of the Act. That application has been received as Exhibit 2 in the case. In accord with 8 C.F.R. section 208.10(b), the application was forwarded to the State Department for its review. The State Department's letter appears as Exhibit 3 in the case. The letter was admitted into evidence over the objection of the respondent's attorney. The Court has admitted this document as required by law. The content of the letter, in the Court's opinion, goes to weight and not admissibility.

The respondent, through her attorney, admitted the truth of the allegations on the Order to Show Cause, conceded deportability, and declined to designate a country of deportation. The undersigned Immigration Judge designated El Salvador. The Order to Show Cause is marked as Exhibit 1 in the case and has been admitted into evidence.

Exhibit 4 is a composite exhibit submitted by the respondent; the first document is entitled "Americas Watch." These documents have been admitted into evidence. Exhibit 5 includes an article from the *Arizona Republic* newspaper, together with two other documents, and has been admitted into evidence. Both Exhibits, 4 and 5, were admitted without objection.

To be eligible for withholding of deportation under section 243(h) of the Act, an applicant's case must demonstrate a clear probability of persecution in the country designated for deportation on account of race, religion, nationality, membership in a particular social group or political opinion. *INS v. Stevic,* 104 S.Ct. 2489 (1984) and *Bolaños-Hernández v. INS,* 749 F.2d 1316 (9th Cir. 1984). This means that the facts of the applicant's case must establish that it is probable that she would be persecuted for one or more of the specific reasons. *(INS v. Stevic).*

To be eligible for asylum under section 208(a) of the Act, an applicant must fit the definition of a refugee, which requires her to show persecution or a well-founded fear of persecution in her homeland on account of race, religion, nationality, membership in a particular social group or political opinion. Section 101(a)(42)(A) of the Act. The Ninth Circuit has concluded that the well-founded fear standard and the clear probability standard are meaningfully different and that the former is more generous than the latter. *Cardoza-Fonseca v. INS,* 767 F.2d 1448 (9th Cir. 1985), *Bolaños-Hernández v. INS.* In describing the amount and type of proof required to establish that a fear of persecution is well-founded, the Ninth Circuit held:

> Applicants must point to specific objective facts that support an inference of past persecution or risk of future persecution. The fact that the objective facts are established through the credible testimony of the applicant does not make those facts less objective. Mere affirmations of possible fear are still insufficient. *Shoaee v. INS,* 704 F.2d 1079 (9th Cir. 1983).

It is only after concrete evidence sufficient to suggest a risk of persecution has been presented that the applicant's subjective fears and desire to avoid the risk-laden situation in his homeland become relevant.

The evidence appears, frankly, to establish a case for the husband more than for the respondent. There is no testimony that the respondent was ever threatened for any of the reasons established by the Act while in her native land.

In addition, it is noted that all family members apparently are well. It is doubtless certain that these people live under conditions of war, which according to the news are improving every day; nevertheless, I do not believe, based on the evidence I have heard, that this respondent has met the requirements for asylum.

There is evidence, obviously, of economic motivations which have been presented by the Trial Attorney. The respondent earned a dollar a day in the fields of El Salvador whereas now she earns $3.35 an hour in this country. This evidence, in my opinion, is irrelevant to the essential matters that have been developed with respect to the asylum case itself.

The respondent has requested voluntary departure in lieu of deportation as an alternative remedy. That application will be granted by the Court.

Based on the respondent's admissions, I find that she is deportable on the charge contained in the Order to Show Cause. The following order will be issued in this case:

ORDER

IT IS HEREBY ORDERED that the respondent's application for asylum under section 208(a) of the Act be denied.

IT IS FURTHER ORDERED that her application for withholding of deportation under section 243(h) of the Act be denied.

IT IS FURTHER ORDERED that the respondent be granted voluntary departure without expense to the government within 31 days of the date of this decision or any extension beyond that date granted by the District Director, under the conditions that she may set.

IT IS FURTHER ORDERED that if the respondent fails to depart when and as required, that the privilege of voluntary departure be revoked and that without further warning or proceedings the following order will immediately become effective: The respondent shall be deported to El Salvador on the charge contained on the Order to Show Cause . . .

Ms. Smith, do you reserve your right to appeal?

Ms. SMITH: Yes, Your Honor.

JUDGE: Thank you. Mr. Hammer?

TRIAL ATTORNEY: No, Your Honor.

JUDGE: Case remains open. Respondent reserves her right to appeal. Case continued.

56

(Kitchen. Calixto, Juancho.)

What's going on with you, Juancho? You haven't said a word all afternoon. Cat got your tongue? What's the deal, man?

(Juancho, grumpily.) Nothing.

Are you sick?

No.

Hm, I think something bad is happening and you don't want to tell me. As if we weren't friends! Remember we're cousins and we go way back. I'm always willing to help you with your problems.

Thanks, Calixto, but I don't need anything.

Did someone die?

No.

And how's everything going with your girlfriend, the *gringuita*?

Okay, more or less.

What do you mean by that? Good or bad?

Okay.

Aha! She's mad at you, isn't she?

(Juancho sighs.) No.

Did she stand you up?

What's that?

That's what you call it when a woman goes off with another man.

What about when the man goes off with another woman?

Same thing.

(Juancho, curious.) And when the man goes off with another man?

It's called the same thing, I guess.

Well, I'm not sure, but last night when we went to a party something like that happened.

She went off with another woman?!

Come on!

Well, explain yourself then. Get to the point!

What happened is, instead of talking to me, she did just the opposite. She spent the whole time talking and dancing with other guys, like I wasn't even there!

Maybe she got tired of talking in sign language, since you don't speak English and she doesn't speak Spanish.

We've always understood each other, using gestures and the words we know, but last night was different.

And how did you feel?

Really strange, confused. Like she doesn't accept me as I am anymore.

What happened at the end of the party?

She just said a friend, a man, was going to take her home.

And what did you do?

I was mad. I just walked away and got into my car.

The Trans Am?

Yeah, at top speed all the way down 16th Street, like a bat out of Hell.

Son-of-a . . . !

Until the police stopped me and gave me a ticket. I have to go to court in two weeks. I imagine I'll have to pay a fine, for being such a fool.

If they don't take away your license.

That's for sure.

And after that, what did you do?

I went back to the apartment and, since everyone who lives there was working, there was nobody to talk to. Then I started to feel really bad and I drank three six-packs of beer.

Eighteen beers! What a binge!

Yeah, man, with the stereo on full blast, listening to that song that goes:

You were deceived, my honest heart,
you gave your love to a wicked woman.

I think the problem is that you fell in love with her, but she didn't fall in love with you. And it doesn't work that way.

(*Juancho continues singing.*)

She swore she loved you madly,
and today she says "I don't love you," sadly . . .

Don't worry, Juancho. I'm going to take you to see someone who just arrived in this country; she just crossed the border a few days ago. She's from Ojo de Agua; you know her.

(*Juancho, suddenly interested.*) Who is she?

One of my wife's cousins.

Not Trinidad?

No, her name is Azucena.

Ah, Ermigia's sister!

That's the one.

She's pretty!

Well she just got here.

Where does she live?

In Springfield, Maryland.

Well, when are we going?

Hold on! Latinas aren't easy. You have to take it slow with them, especially when they still have the customs from back home.

That's for sure. They're skittish.

Shy but good!

(*They laugh. Juancho finally regains his typical good humor and jocularity.*) But when are we going? Don't make this so hard on me!

Okay, tomorrow.

Great! I hope no one beats me to her.

If it's meant to be, it's meant to be.

(*The two friends continue washing the dirty dishes that had accumulated into an enormous pile. It's Saturday, the busiest day, when they usually work until 3 a.m.*)

57

Compañero Tzi-Vihán:

I write this letter although I know it is too late for it to reach your hands. I write it with the ink of my tears, on the way to the airport, to catch the plane that will return me to our land. I know that this is exactly what I should not do because I am a marked woman and my life is in danger, but now I also understand that it was a serious mistake to have ever left your side, that it would have been better to stay and face the consequences, since that too is part of the struggle.

I have broken the promise of not returning to my country because you also broke your promise that you would wait for me. You've gone to the great beyond, leaving me alone and vulnerable, like thousands of our children. That is why I am returning, because my destiny is my homeland, because breathing the air of our land I will be breathing you, I will be near your spirit.

I will continue the struggle in your memory. Because as long as I continue fighting, you will live. That is why I am going back. For you, *Compañero* Tzi-Vihán. Because I am going to offer my life to my people, and perhaps I will have the good fortune to die with the same honors as you did, and be reunited then with you, in the great beyond, at the right hand of Tepeu and Gucumatz.

Wait for me, my love. I will be with you soon.

"The people will overcome."

Tzu-Nihá

58

The guide and driver from the vehicle in which Calixto's group was travelling after crossing the border were also detained in El Corralón.

The driver had suffered harsh treatment at the time of his arrest. His shirt was ripped off and he was made to walk barefoot through the desert, in spite of the fact that it was bitterly cold.

It was the second time he had been arrested for smuggling undocumented persons. The authorities tried to make a deal with him. They promised to set him free if he would reveal who his contacts were. From that moment on he had not been heard from again until a few days later when he appeared in El Corralón. He immediately struck up a friendship with Charro and Turk. Calixto and the soldier guessed that possibly the three already knew each other.

Another curious character was Priest, who had been a seminarian. Often he would suddenly begin to preach, as if illuminated. At mealtime he would pray aloud, over the booing and insults of the other detainees. He always had a Bible under his arm.

Once a week religious evangelists came to El Corralón to preach "the word of God" and teach Christian principles to the detainees. At the beginning of each session, a small group that included Priest would be listening attentively, but after ten minutes many lost interest and left. At the end Priest and the evangelists were the only ones left, immersed in complicated arguments about the existence of God.

There was a deep feeling of solidarity among the prisoners, especially among the Latin Americans. At night, after the lights were turned off, they would tell each other their life stories.

One group of Mexicans had the habit of singing softly at night, and their sad songs filled the dark dormitory, rekindling everyone's longing for home and loved ones, far away, south of the border. They would sing *ranchera* songs, and the most popular one, "The Swallow," was like the national anthem of those prisoners, its words heard every night:

I wonder where the swallow, swift but weary,
will go now that it has taken flight,
flying against the wind, anguished,
searching for shelter it will not find.
Next to my bed I will place its nest,
oh Holy Heaven, and it will not find it.
I too am lost in the season,
oh Holy Heaven, unable to fly.

The detainees quietly related to each other their personal stories, testimonies that spoke of fragmented families and abandoned homes, of journeys, filled with thousands of trials and tribulations, that few managed to complete and finally enter the longed-for paradise of the North.

The whispering of the prisoners and their stories often ended at two o'clock in the morning. It seemed that each and every one of them felt the urgent need to tell something. Silence was their worst enemy; it ate them up inside and caused them to despair. Therefore, solidarity and understanding were their highest expressions of friendship. Everyone needed someone to talk to.

59

(A crowded, noisy bar. Juancho, Calixto and Caremacho are conversing happily. The jukebox is playing rancheras, cumbias, boleros *and* merengues. *The patrons, mainly young and undocumented, drink beer, tell jokes, and kid around with each other, but without becoming too distracted. They must be ready to take off running through the closest door if the feared Immigration agents appear or if some drunken person starts to throw bottles and chairs and starts a fight. They have to shout to be heard, so their stories, each more unbelievable than the last, are not told in vain. There is no shortage of flirting with the waitresses and, among friends, the rude insults accompanied by their respective denigrating nicknames. Drinks are demanded and offered; they argue about details that matter to no one but that, nevertheless, must be defended with heated arguments and, if all else fails, resorting to fists. Even in these distant lands, among these people it is popular consensus that being Latino means not giving in, regardless of the consequences. At Calixto's table the discussion revolves around the year soon to end and plans for the approaching New Year.)*

(Juancho, after draining his glass of beer, burps loudly and apologizes with a heavily-accented English "Excuse me.") I've been in this country a year already and nothing's changed. Since I don't speak English, I can't get a good job.

I have a tough time too, washing dishes, pots and pans. One of the days I hate most is Friday.

Yeah. Fridays we have to go in at three in the afternoon and work non-stop 'til three in the morning.

When I'm finished, I'm dead-tired and my feet are swollen. Besides that, I'm drunk, because the boss makes us drink beer after beer so we get warmed up and work like dogs.

When I finally fall into bed, I don't ever want to get up again.

Yeah, but we have to get up early to work Saturday.

And Saturday is worse yet.

Dishwashing is a hard job. But it's the easiest job to find.

They say all Washington restaurants have at least one Salvadoran dishwasher. We've got the reputation of being hard workers.

Reputation of being slaves, you mean. Because we'll do anything. We don't turn up our noses at anything.

(*Juancho, enthused.*) Let's have another drink. To the New Year.

Or to the old.

To any one. The thing is to have the drink!

A few days ago one of my friends was almost caught by the *migra*. Somebody had reported him. But he escaped from two agents who had him cornered.

Your friend is really slick!

But he couldn't go back to where he lived because he thought they'd go looking for him there. And a few days later when he went by to pick up his things, he found they had thrown them out into the street.

So where did he go?

He came to the apartment where I live, to see if we could rent him a little corner to sleep in. There are forty of us living there.

Forty! How can so many people live in one apartment?

We live there in shifts. The people who work days go there at night to sleep, and those who work nights sleep there during the day.

So really only twenty people live there.

That's right. Twenty during the day and twenty at night.

How confusing!

Well, anyway, the friend I'm talking about was in luck, because the day before, Immigration had caught one of the people who lived there, so there was room in the closet where he slept. The owner rented it to him right away.

A closet? You can't fit anything in a closet! How can a man sleep there?

The owner of the apartment put a small bed in there. And my friend is happy because he only pays a hundred-and-fifty dollars a month. A bargain!

It's been a year since I crossed the Río Grande.

The Río Grande or the Río Bravo?

It's the same one. On the Mexican side they call it Bravo and on this side Grande. It's like crossing two rivers.

That's how it seems.

So you've been a wetback for a whole year now, Calixto.

We'll have to sing "Happy Birthday"!

(*Calixto, trying to ignore his friends' jokes.*) And I've tried quite a few jobs: washing windows, cleaning offices, washing dishes, gardening, painting apartments, I've even worked in construction.

Me, I'm planning to go back home next year. Even if we have nothing to eat but beans, I just want to be home.

But you can't do anything in our country now. There are no jobs. Here, even if you work like a beast of burden, at least you're employed.

Maybe the New Year will bring us better luck. That's when I'm planning to go to school to learn English and see if that way I can get a better job.

Maybe things will get straightened out in El Salvador and we can go back.

I think we'd better have another beer.

Fine with me.

Cheers!

Here's to you not washing so many dishes next year!

Cheers!

Here's to you not cleaning so many toilets!

Cheers!

Here's to you marrying a *gringa* and getting your green card!

Cheers!

To the New Year!

Cheers!

(*From the back of the bar someone suddenly shouts: "Long live Latin America!" Immediately everyone stands, raising bottles and glasses to chorus "Qué viva!" For a moment a feeling of brotherhood is felt in the crowded bar. Those gathered there suddenly remember that they are united by a common destiny and that, although poverty and violence afflict their countries, those places will never cease to be their beloved homelands, something that nothing and no one, not even distance, can take away from them. From the jukebox, meanwhile, comes the strong voice of Tony Camargo.)*

I won't forget the old year
because it has left me many good things,
it left me a goat, an old donkey,
a white mare and a good mother-in-law.

60

BODY OF WOMAN FOUND

The remains of a woman have been found near Cantón El Jocote, San Miguel. Local authorities identified her as twenty-one-year-old Teresa de Jesús Delgado. According to information gathered from neighbors, the deceased had recently been deported from the United States for having entered that country without legal documents. It is believed that her death was due to political retaliation.

La Tribuna
San Salvador
October 14, 1986

61

Calixto, José and the soldier were released at noon. Their names were called over the loudspeakers, telling them to report to the office. They were given a certificate indicating their bonds had been paid. Their passports, however, were kept by the Immigration authorities. Then the main gate to the prison was opened, they were taken outside and the enormous iron door closed behind them.

"It's like when you go out of the movie theater," said José, "from complete darkness into the light of day."

Taxis were usually waiting at the gate, along with volunteers from community organizations that provided assistance to the former inmates, since they were completely disoriented upon release. But that day the street was deserted, and Calixto and company began to walk away from the prison.

"Juancho paid my bond and Toño paid yours," Calixto told José. "And they paid for our tickets on a flight that leaves at two o'clock this afternoon from the El Paso airport to Atlanta, Georgia."

"How do you know?" asked José.

"Before we left, they let me use the phone in the office to call Juancho," stated Calixto.

The soldier explained, "My brother, who lives in Silver Spring, Maryland, paid my bond, and also made me a reservation on a flight to Washington, but I'm not sure what time it leaves."

"Maybe it's the same flight we're on," said Calixto.

"It's possible," said the soldier. "So we can go to the airport together."

"Great," said José, "but how do we get to the airport?"

"My brother told me that I should be at the airport at least two hours before the flight leaves," said the soldier, "to find the airline, get my ticket and board before two o'clock."

"This is a big problem," said Calixto. "We're free but we don't know how to make use of our freedom."

The three stood for a moment in the middle of the street, not knowing what to do. Then they saw two people waving and calling to them as they emerged from another part of the prison. It was Silvia and Elisa. They waved back and the women joined them.

"Together again," said the soldier with emotion.

"My husband paid the bond for both of us," said Silvia. "He lives in Virginia. He bought us a ticket on a flight to Atlanta and from there to Washington."

"That's where we're going too!" exclaimed José.

"What a coincidence!" observed Silvia. "It's like all our relatives got together and decided to get us out of jail on the same day."

"The attorney helped us a lot," Elisa reminded them. "Without her we might still be in prison."

"This trip has been a real adventure," said Calixto. "Never in my life would I have imagined that I was going to go through all the things that have happened to us."

They could not find a way to get to the airport, and they did not have a cent in their pockets to pay for a taxi. So they decided to return to the prison, where they pounded on the gate until a guard came out. Calixto explained, "We're lost. We don't know how to get to the airport!"

The officer, without opening the gate, returned to his desk and picked up the phone. Meanwhile, time was passing. The clock at El Corralón showed 1 p.m. The plane was leaving at 2 and they were still at the prison gate!

Finally the man came out and said, "Don't worry, I'll take you myself."

They jumped into his car and rushed directly to the airport.

"It's not common for us to do things like this," said the guard, a man of Colombian origin, "but I could see you were in a tight spot and I don't want you to miss your flight."

Once inside the airport, Immigration agents noticed them and approached them with the intention of arresting them, but left them alone after checking the documents they received at El Corralón and after the guard who was accompanying them explained the situation to his fellow officers.

Calixto and company bore the seal of the undocumented. They were still wearing the same clothes as when they started their trip. Finally, with the officer's help, they got their tickets and managed to board the plane on time.

The plane made a stop in Atlanta, and from there they flew to Washington, D.C.'s National Airport, arriving later that night.

They got off the plane and entered the airport concourse. A group of people was waiting in the baggage claim area. Silvia saw her husband, ran to him, and they embraced. "You can't imagine what we've gone through to get here," she said, her eyes full of tears.

Juancho and Toño were waiting in the corner of the room, and José shouted, "Juancho, Toño, here we are!" They ran to greet their cousins with a strong embrace.

"Wow," said Toño, "you guys look like you've had a real scare!"

"I think it was worse than that," said Calixto. "These last few days have been the hardest days of my life!"

The soldier had found his brother and they were conversing, with great emotion, in the concourse.

"This trip was sure an incredible adventure," said the soldier.

"Yes, but you're here now," said his brother. "Now you can start a new life."

"I don't have much time," explained the soldier. "In a few months I have to go to Immigration Court and they'll decide my case. I hope they don't deport me."

"Forget that," said the brother. "Most people don't even show up for court."

"But then they'll issue an arrest warrant. And we'll lose the bond money."

"Among so many millions of people they'll never find you. And you can pay me back the bond money whenever you can. The important thing is that you made it."

The traveling companions said their goodbyes to each other and departed with their relatives in different directions.

"Welcome to the United States!" Silvia's husband said to the two women. "Thank God you made it and we're together again."

"You can't imagine how hard the trip was," said Elisa.

"I can imagine," said Silvia's husband. "Don't forget I came to this country the same way. But I want you to tell me everything, anyway."

Silvia and her husband, followed by Elisa, left the airport and headed for the parking lot.

Calixto, José and their cousins caught a taxi to take them to the city and, as they talked about the journey, Calixto leaned back in the seat, breathed deeply and closed his eyes.

The memory of his home filled his thoughts again. He walked the streets, greeted the friends he usually met along the way, entered the poor apartment complex and then the room where his wife waited with dinner on the table. The beans and tortillas, their usual delicious smell. Calixto watched Lina and thought how his wife still kept her attractive figure in spite of the years, the work and the worries about the children. The children were playing out in the yard.

He opened his eyes and before his weary gaze stretched the highway along the Potomac River that separated Virginia from Washington. The blurred images of home refused to leave his memory, and Calixto thought, "Really, I'm not far from my people or my home. I have them as close to my heart as if I had never left them."

July 1983-May 1998

About the Author

Mario Bencastro, author and playwright, was born in Ahuachapán, El Salvador, in 1949. His first novel, *A Shot in the Cathedral*, was chosen from among 204 works as a finalist in the Novedades y Diana International Literary Prize 1989 in Mexico, and was published by Editorial Diana in 1990.

In 1988 his play *Crossroad* was performed by the Hispanic Cultural Society Theater Group at Thomas Jefferson Theater in Arlington, Virginia. This play was also chosen for Georgetown University's Bicentennial Festival for the Performing Arts in 1989.

In 1993 his short story collection *The Tree of Life: Stories of Civil War* was published in El Salvador under the direction of Editorial Clásicos Roxsil. Written between 1979 and 1990, several of these stories have been included in international anthologies.

"Photographer of Death" and "Clown's Story" have been adapted for the stage. The latter was translated into English for the anthologies *Where Angels Glide at Dawn* (HarperCollins 1990) and *Turning Points* (Nelson Canada, 1993). "Photographer of Death" is included in *Texto y vida: Introducción a la literatura hispanoamericana* (Harcourt Brace, 1992) and in *Voces: Vistas del mundo hispánico* (Prentice Hall, 1994). "The River Goddess" is part of *Antología 3 X 5 mundos: Cuentos salvadoreños 1962-1992* (UCA Editores, San Salvador, 1994). "The Garden of Gucumatz" was first published in *Hispanic Cultural Review* (George Mason University, 1994).

In 1994 his short novel *The Flight of the Lark* was a finalist in the Felipe Trigo Literary Prize competition in Badajoz, Spain.

Arte Público Press published *A Shot in the Cathedral* in English and in Spanish (*Disparo en la catedral*) in 1996, *The Tree of Life: Stories of Civil War* in English and in Spanish (*Árbol de la vida: Historias de la guerra civil*) in 1997, and *Odisea del Norte* in 1999.

About the Translator

Susan Giersbach Rascón, an attorney, from 1983 to 1989 represented Central American refugees, most of them Salvadoran, in their attempts to gain political asylum in the United States. Since 1990 she has taught Spanish at Lawrence University in Appleton, Wisconsin, where she created and taught a course titled "Art and Social Responsibility: The Works of Mario Bencastro." She has also translated Mr. Bencastro's novel *A Shot in the Cathedral* and his short story collection *The Tree of Life: Stories of Civil War* (both published by Arte Público Press). She has presented bilingual readings and papers on Mr. Bencastro's works at conferences in the United States, Costa Rica, El Salvador, Guatemala, and Panama.